THE CROW'S NEST

BY BARBARA GILES

BeeJayGee Press
Florence, Oregon

This novel is entirely a work of fiction. The names, characters, and incidents portrayed in it are the work of the author's imagination. Any similarity to real persons, living or dead, is coincidental, and not intended by the author.

Published by BeeJayGee Press
Florence, Oregon

ISBN: 1494258315

Cover by Pattie Brooks Anderson
www.pattiebrooksanderson.com

This book is lovingly dedicated to my mom, Dorothy Giles, who always inspired me to write as she is a writer herself, and to my daughter, Sarah Brown, who has blessed my life in so many ways. She shares all her good reads with me and encouraged me to publish this book.

THE CROW'S NEST

Chapter One

As she stepped out of her silver Lexus SUV, Julie could hear the surf pounding wildly behind the house situated in the midst of the dunes. With the wind whipping at her shoulder-length, gray-blonde hair, she was smiling for the first time in ages. Her hazel eyes sparkled with excitement. This was going to be a great listing. Waterfront property always sold well, even in this economy. A picket fence contained a charming garden with a stone path leading to the front door. Although the cottage was probably built in the twenties, the gray-blue paint was fresh as was the white trim. When she looked up and saw the crow's nest perched on top of the second floor, she couldn't wait to get inside.

Unlocking the red door with the key the out-of-town owners had sent, she gave a cursory glance to the downstairs. Julie's childhood memories of the rental beach house her family had leased one summer compelled her up to the crow's nest. As she quickly mounted the stairs, she remembered a room that was cozy when the fog wafted around the windows, where, even when her parents were fighting, she felt at peace. It was the last time her family had been together. Her parents divorced shortly afterwards.

She entered the third-floor room and looked around. With windows centered on each of the four walls, she had almost a 360° view of the dunes and ocean. Floor-to-ceiling bookcases bracketed one side window. All four window sills held beach treasures of sea glass, shells, starfish, and sand dollars. As she picked up a piece of blue glass, she held her breath remembering when she'd collected such bits of beauty as a child. She'd waited her whole life for another room like this.

Even with the windows closed, the surf roared in her ears. For the first time in months, she felt at peace. She settled on the blue and white quilt-covered sofa in front of the beachside window and corner fireplace. She closed her eyes. *I've finally come home,* she thought, realizing she'd subconsciously dreamed of owning a room like this since that summer she was ten.

Not so, her recent ex-husband, Ted. Ted had loved only the very modern, the shiny, glass and metal look--very minimalist. He was a decorator and was insistent that he knew best. It was important that their home reflect his talent and taste. Their condo, penthouse level, was gorgeous, modern, and cold. He never gave in on anything, including the decor of their sterile home. But now . . .

Although she mourned the loss of Ted and the bitterness of the divorce, Julie felt that she could heal in a room like this--she could rediscover her identity. As she got up and opened the window closest to the surf, she breathed in the fresh sea air and watched as the breeze fluttered papers on the desk. Though not a large room, it held everything she could ever want in a refuge--a desk on which to write, a blue and white striped wing-back chair with ottoman from which to view the ocean, dream, and read, a sofa for napping or occasionally entertaining, a fireplace, a telescope, shelves for books. In one corner, she even found a tiny fridge and hot plate. She could live up here for days! And, since this cottage had been used as a vacation home, it even came fully furnished.

Yes, this was it. She wasn't going to list this house. She was going to buy it. Maybe by the end of the month she'd be living here. Julie inhaled the salty breeze again, closed the window, and set off to investigate the rest of the house. It really didn't matter; she'd already decided. Bedrooms were bedrooms, kitchens were kitchens, bathrooms were bathrooms, but a crow's nest . . . rare perfection.

Once back in her real estate office in town, Julie realized that ethically she couldn't put in an offer until the house had been appraised. She really should have a colleague arrange that so she wouldn't be accused of low-balling her prospective clients. So she went in to see the lead broker and explained the situation to her. Once she had her broker's approval, she called the Thompsons in Arizona and shared her position with them.

They were quite happy to have a buyer without the hassle of having to repeatedly show the house and were very willing to cooperate. They said that once the appraisal came in, they would be happy to discuss her offer. Julie was in a better state than she had been in for more than a year. How her marriage had dragged her down. She actually hadn't realized how depressed she was, staying in that god-awful condo until she found her own space. Ted would buy her out. And now she'd found the perfect home--it really was a home not just a place in which to live.

Ted had temporarily moved in with his assistant, the charming, young Tina. Their affair had been going on for most of the last three of the twenty years Julie was married to Ted. But Julie'd been in complete denial. That is, until Tina divorced her husband and was free. Then Ted, anxious to live with Tina, had "fessed up"-- the louse. Julie had dreamed that when she married, it would be forever. But obviously she couldn't keep something together when Ted had already left.

She dialed Ted.

"Ted, I've found a place I want to buy."

"You know you could keep the condo longer if you need it," he said. "I can stay with Tina. Where'd you find a condo so quickly in the city?"

"What? No, it isn't in the city. And it's not a condo; it's a house--at the beach." She waited for the criticism sure to follow.

"Are you sure you want to live in that climate? It's probably old and drafty. I can lend you some money, plus you get my buy-out for your half of the condo, if you want to buy a new place."

Julie groaned. Ted didn't get it. He would never understand why she would want to live anywhere but the city. And he certainly couldn't comprehend an old house when he so valued the new, the shiny. Interestingly, his guilt over his affair made him feel that he should offer to help her out financially. No way. She wanted to do this on her own. It was about time. Besides, she had plenty of money. That was not going to be an issue.

"Listen, Ted. I plan to be out of the condo in about a month. I just wanted to give you a head's up. When I have more details, I'll let you know. Bye for now."

She sat at her desk and looked around the office. She actually had a nice corner desk with a window view of downtown. Her space had been personalized with a few photographs of Ted, which she'd since removed. Now her Real Estate License, a photo she'd taken at the beach, and a coastal watercolor a friend had painted were all that she had on the walls. Her books and reference materials were on the small walnut bookcase under the window.

She leaned back and surveyed her desk. Just her laptop, an appointment calendar (she never could learn to rely on an electronic calendar), a small vase of sweet peas, and a cup filled with pens and pencils were displayed on the broad expanse of her walnut desk. It was an uncluttered view so that when her clients sat across from her, things didn't get in the way. She'd enjoyed working here while she lived in the city. But now, maybe it was time to transfer to their sister office on the coast. Wouldn't it be wonderful to work and live by the sea?

Although she'd spent time on the warm beaches of southern California as a child, especially the summer they'd rented the crow's nest house, as an adult, she'd grown to appreciate the wilder beaches of northern California and Oregon. She loved wearing sweatshirts and jeans on the beach or slickers when it rained. She hadn't gone to the coast nearly enough once she met Ted. She didn't think he liked the sand in his shoes or the wind blowing his hair, the way she did. He was more of a palm trees and tropics beach goer. He enjoyed Maui where they'd gone on their honeymoon. She didn't care for the oppressive humidity and warm temperatures. It had been pleasant and lovely, but she wouldn't want to live there. She wanted rough, noisy oceans with winter storms--cool weather. Oh, this was going to be perfect.

She'd been lucky that the Thompsons had called her at this branch. They were referred to her specifically by one of her cousins. Otherwise the cottage probably would have been listed by a broker on the coast, and she would've never seen it. *My crow's nest.* It was all she could think about.

Her phone rang waking her from her trance. Time to get back to work.

"Julie Maxwell," she answered, thinking how glad she was she'd kept her own name. She wouldn't need to change it back with the divorce. "How may I help you?"

She put her dreams on hold as she talked with one of her clients about his house which was closing in a few days.

In a week's time, the appraisal on the crow's nest had been completed, and the Thompsons had accepted her offer. Her loan was in the works, and Ted had come through with her half of the condo's value. Soon she would be living at the beach--a new life for a new person. It was all she could do to return to the condo at night. She'd begun a countdown--twenty more days and she would start over.

Chapter Two

The weeks had passed quickly. It was Sunday evening, her first night in her new home, as she sat on the sofa in the crow's nest sipping Cognac. She'd lit a fire in the fireplace; the weather had cooperated. It was a gorgeous foggy evening with the distant sound of a foghorn bleeping for company.

What an easy move, she thought. She'd only had to move her personal belongings--no furniture, linens, or kitchenware. Her cottage had all the essentials, so she'd left nearly everything behind for Ted. She needed no reminders of the condo or him in this, her new home.

Julie glanced out the window and reveled in her new dwelling. Her bedroom below was one of two on the second floor. With a spectacular view of the ocean through a large picture window and with a good-sized closet, this room was going to suit her wonderfully. She should sleep well tonight with the surf as her lullaby--if she ever got up from this comfortable sofa.

Each of the two bedrooms on the second floor had its own bath. They'd probably been remodeled in the last ten years from a three bedroom, one bath original build. She'd discovered that all the rooms had been freshly painted and were in good repair. It was better than she'd dreamed. No renovation needed. As soon as she'd finished making up her bed and unpacking, she'd gone down to the kitchen and fixed dinner.

After stir-frying some vegetables in the well-equipped kitchen and doing the dishes, she'd grabbed her bottle of Cognac and climbed the stairs. And now she was soothed by the fire and the fog in her new retreat.

Too bad she had to go to work the next day. However, she'd only be commuting to the city for no longer than a month, and not even daily, as she finished up assisting her few remaining clients. Then she would transfer to the beach office. It was all working out without a hitch. Ted could go to hell. Her life was better than ever. In fact, maybe she should thank him, she mused, as she sipped from her snifter.

It hadn't always been bad. She'd been flattered, when tall, handsome Ted had asked her out. Actually they'd met at a condo she'd listed that needed staging. Ted, an up-and-coming designer, had been referred to her, and he'd done an excellent job decorating the loft-like structure. She liked his poise and self-confidence, not to mention his strong jaw and startling emerald eyes framed by his dark brunette hair. He'd seemed taken with her as well. He'd wined and dined her, taken her to the theatre. They'd had a wonderful time. He seemed intent on winning her, something that was new to her. She'd always seemed to be the one who tried to do the pleasing in most of her previous relationships.

It hadn't lasted. Gradually, once they were married, he gained control. When they'd eventually purchased their prize condo ten years ago, he'd been the one who'd chosen the penthouse and the furniture. They ate dinner at restaurants he liked. He even confessed that he hated the theatre, but because he knew she loved it, he'd taken her to shows to court her. He said he no longer needed to go places he didn't like because he'd arrived. He didn't need to impress anyone, inferring even her. She was his now, and he knew it. Ted understood how she felt about fighting and discord after her parents' divorce. He knew she wouldn't demand things or leave him. She was surprised by what a different person he'd become over the years. Or maybe this was who he'd always been, only she hadn't wanted to see it.

The world revolved around him--his genius, his talent, his work. He said that he had a real career, and she couldn't possibly understand the work of an artist. Although he had never objected to the money she brought in, especially when she'd made a big sale and received a really large commission during those early years. He said her work was something anybody could do--a realtor--just a job. His required talent.

She got tired of massaging his ego and found more clients and more excuses to stay at work. They didn't have real friends. Ted liked an audience around him. Therefore, the people they saw were those who could help his career. She was lonely but not sure what to do about it, so she worked more hours. It paid off. She was quite successful, but she felt adrift.

It really was no wonder that he became enthralled with Tina. She worshipped him as only an assistant to an artist can. He called her his muse. Soon the muse was sharing his bed, unbeknownst to Julie, who kept plugging along, still earning a decent portion of their income. His talent was real though, and since the tenth year of their marriage, he'd begun earning good money, too, often surpassing her. That's probably when he began to lose interest. He didn't need her to support him any longer.

Julie refilled her glass as she recalled the night he told her about Tina. It was one of the worst in her life (maybe only second to the night her parents had informed her of their decision to divorce).

Enough of this, she told herself. *You're living in the crow's nest now. Life will be different.*

She found her way to bed about two a.m., but got up in time to make her drive to the office in the city. The week passed quickly with five days of commuting as she wound down her work there. Although the scenery was beautiful through the mountains, she would be grateful to be at the beach full-time.

* * * * * * * * * *

Now, after enjoying her first full week at the coast, Julie at age fifty-five felt that she had finally found her true home. Friday night she'd spent looking at the stars from the crow's nest on a beautiful, clear evening with a full moon. She was mesmerized by the sound of the waves and the enchanting view of the silver moon reflected in the water. Luminous light seemed to shoot straight towards her through the window. It was magical.

She'd slept in until nine Saturday morning. Now she was sipping coffee in her blue and white kitchen, sitting at the tiny table that overlooked the street. From her window, she could see three other homes spaced out in the dunes. She knew there were more, but no others were visible from this window. She would venture out this morning, walking through the neighborhood to see if anybody was around. She hoped they weren't all vacation homes. It would be nice to have some real neighbors.

The doorbell rang. She peered through the glass and saw two women standing on her porch. She hurried to the door and opened it.

"Hi," they chimed in unison.

The brunette, tall and thin with a long pony tail, appeared to be a little younger than Julie, probably in her mid-forties. "We're neighbors," she said. "Hi, I'm Jenn and this is Eleanor." She pointed to a lovely woman with a gray bob and soft blue eyes who looked timeless, but was probably in her sixties.

"Hi," she replied. "I'm Julie. Won't you come in?"

"Are you sure it won't be a problem?" Eleanor asked in a soft British accent. "We brought you home-made muffins that Jenn just baked. I supplied the marmalade. We just wanted to welcome you to the neighborhood."

"They look delicious," Julie responded. "And it's no problem whatsoever. I just made coffee. Please come in," she added as she moved aside. "The kitchen's to your right."

They stood at the breakfast bar as Julie said, "This is so perfect. I was going to take a walk around the neighborhood a little later and try to get acquainted, and here you are. How would you like your coffees?"

They told her, and she quickly fixed them each a cup which she then placed on a tray with the muffins and marmalade. " Let's sit in the living room," she motioned.

As they enjoyed their coffee and muffins, she discovered that Jenn and Eleanor lived next door to each other further down the street. Jenn, a sculptor, was married; Eleanor, retired, was also divorced. They shared basic information about a few of the other neighbors and invited her to go with them to the farmer's market Sunday. She agreed to join them

While washing the plates and cups after they left, she thought how fortunate she was to be making new friends already. So different from life in the city.

An hour later, Julie was traipsing over the dunes on the path from her house to the beach. It was a beautiful day out with just a bit of a breeze--perfect walking weather. She nodded and said hello to several children building sand castles, to a handsome man walking his black lab, and to several couples also strolling. She found some gorgeous blue-green sea glass, two pieces, to add to the window-sill collection.

As she hiked back up over the dunes, contentment spread throughout her body. She really was at peace.

If only it would last.

She opened the patio door to the living room just as the phone began to ring. "Hello," she answered.

"Hi Julie, this is Eleanor."

"Hi Eleanor. So good to hear from you."

"I'm planning a small party tonight. I thought you'd like to meet some of our neighbors. I hope you can come."

"Tonight?" Julie answered. "I'd love to. May I bring something--maybe some wine?"

"That would be great. My house is down the street--the yellow one, number 63. Will five o'clock work for you?"

"Sure. Thanks, Eleanor. Sounds like fun. See you then."

Lovely--an invitation to a small gathering at Eleanor's to meet a few more neighbors. She'd bring a great Pinot Gris she'd stashed in the wine cupboard. She grabbed it and put it in the fridge to chill. She forgot to ask about dress but assumed it would be casual. After all, this was the beach, and Eleanor didn't look like the formal type.

Julie spent the afternoon putting away a few more things and arranging the kitchen cupboards to suit her. She loved the china the previous owners left--bright-colored Fiestaware that looked old and was probably original. The pots and pans were pretty worn, and she'd probably need to replace them. But most everything in the kitchen she could use. Glancing at the clock, she saw that it was already four. She should probably bathe and get ready. After all, Eleanor said five o'clock.

Chapter Three

Normally Julie found it hard to be a guest when she really didn't know the others. She'd never mastered small talk. Oh, she had no problem talking with clients because she had a focus. But conversation with strangers could be a strain. However, the hour she'd spent with Eleanor and Jenn that morning over coffee had been quite comfortable. So she was fairly relaxed as she walked over to Eleanor's home, a cute yellow dollhouse. She knocked on the door, which was opened by Eleanor wearing almost an identical sweatshirt and jeans. Good, she'd correctly guessed the clothing style for the party, she thought to herself.

Eleanor ushered her out to the living room facing the ocean and introduced her. "Everyone, this is our delightful new neighbor, Julie. She lives in the house with the crow's nest that none of us even knew was on the market."

Julie nodded. "I fell in love with it before it even got listed."

"Okay," said Eleanor, "I'm going to let you all introduce yourselves."

The good-looking man from the beach was there with Jenn. He was her husband, Robbie. They made a striking couple--both tall, slim, and athletic-looking. She met a husband and wife who were both retired dentists, Bob and Sharon; another single woman, Kerry, a stained-glass artist, who appeared to be about forty; and Phil and Jon, a handsome couple in their mid-forties, she guessed. Everyone was friendly, asked questions, and told her bits about themselves. It looked like she'd found community as well as a home.

She was engaged in a conversation with Robbie and Jenn when she became aware of a presence behind her. She turned and looked into the most astonishing blue eyes she'd ever seen.

"I've just arrived," Mr. Blue Eyes said. "You must be our new neighbor, Julie, the reason for our party tonight. I'm William, friends call me Bill--surfer, beach bum, and entrepreneur. Pleased to meet you."

She sure didn't need another man in her life, but this was one good-looking guy. It was all she could do not to stare at his tanned face with sun-bleached, grayish-auburn hair combed slightly over his forehead, and those incredible eyes. Bill looked like a surfer--much like Robert Redford did before he started looking so old.

"I'm so glad to meet you," she finally said. "Do you surf here?"

"When I'm not in Hawaii or other parts of the world," he replied. "Do you surf?"

"Not since I was a teenager," she answered. "I was never very good at it, but I loved to float on the board out beyond the breakers. It was so soothing. I had some pretty wild rides into the shore. I never really mastered the standing up part of it."

"Well, I'd be happy to teach you, if you're interested," Bill offered.

"I'll keep that in mind," Julie answered. "But the water seems pretty cold here."

"Oh, we wear wetsuits," he said. "Need to fill my glass. See you later."

She watched him walk over to the bar and felt like the sun had just clouded over. *Don't be silly,* she told herself, as she resumed conversation with Jenn and Robbie.

The party broke up about ten, and Phil and Jon, who lived across the street from her, walked her home. It'd been a good evening with such lovely neighbors, she thought. But Bill was going to create problems for her if she wasn't careful. Probably he was just being polite, but before she'd left, he'd said he would call. She wasn't sure she wanted him to. And yet, after she went in her front door, she looked over to the counter at the phone. *He won't call this soon, silly,* she said to herself. And he hadn't.

* * * * * * * * * *

Sunday morning after she'd had a leisurely breakfast, Jenn and Eleanor came by to take her to the farmer's market and art fair on the wharf. As they strolled the stalls, she was introduced to more people than she would ever remember. She had never lived in such a friendly place.

By the time they went to lunch at a darling riverfront cafe, she'd been invited to join a book club, a creative spirits group, a yoga class, and a beach walking group. Since her new job was going to be part-time, not full-time, and since her schedule was a bit negotiable, she hoped to try out all four activities and find out what interested her the most. She was intrigued by the creative spirits group since she never thought of herself as artistic. But Pamela, the woman who invited her, said there were lots of ways to be creative. One did not have to be an artist. It might be fun to explore and see if she had an artistic flair.

Eleanor said, "I hope you'll think about the yoga class. I go twice a week. It's done wonders for my body and my spirit. My back pain is non-existent-- something I'd lived with for years before yoga."

"Plus, you'll meet the most interesting people there," said Jenn. "Men and women, all age groups, although, to be honest, most are about our age."

She was interrupted by Bill who was standing by their table. "I hope I'm one of the most interesting," he said, nodding to Jenn. Then he looked at Julie. "I attend when I'm in town. It would be great to see you at yoga. Sometimes, if the weather is nice, we meet at the beach. Sorry to eavesdrop, but I was just standing here waiting to say hello."

Julie felt herself tense. *He does seem a bit arrogant,* she told herself, *but then he appears to have a lot to be proud of.* Taking a breath, she looked up and said, "Why hi, Bill. How are you today?" *That's pretty lame,* she thought.

"Fine, fine. Well ladies, enjoy your lunch. May I recommend the Margaritas?"

They all said good-by, and Eleanor raised her eyebrows. "My, my," she said, looking at Julie. "I think he's interested in you."

Julie blushed. "Uh, I don't think so. It's just that I'm new in town."

"I think not," Jenn chimed in. "Bill doesn't waste time with people he's not interested in. Do you like him?"

"I don't know him well enough to say yes or no at this point," Julie answered, not mentioning that she'd looked for a phone call after the party.

"Now, about the book club," Julie said, changing the subject. "Tell me, what's the group currently reading?"

"Better than that," Jenn replied. "We'll take you to the bookstore and let you meet the owner and organizer of several book clubs. We meet in her coffeehouse bookstore."

They finished their lunch and then spent an hour walking around the marina and down to the charming shops on the bay front, including the wonderful bookstore. Jandy, the owner, with her big brown eyes, long cornrows, and friendly smile, welcomed her and showed her the list of book clubs. Wow. African studies, women writers, mysteries, sci fi, even romance. Jandy organized all kinds of clubs. Julie picked up the information on the mystery and women authors groups, buying the books that the two groups were reading: the current Sue Grafton for the mystery club, which was going to meet in two weeks, and a Toni Morrison for the women authors, which met in almost a month.

When Julie got home, she was tired and took a nap on the sofa in her crow's nest with the warm sun blanketing her, beaming in the window from over the ocean. She slept peacefully only to be awakened by a phone call from her new realty office.

They had space for her starting on Monday. The agent who'd been using the desk had already left. They asked if she would be willing to start then and just transfer over the work from her city office. She said yes and was so happy that she wouldn't have to make the drive for the rest of the month, except to meet with a couple of clients whose work she was finishing. She really was making a significant change. Her new life was looking wonderful. Who would've guessed she would already have friends and invitations? Small-town living was going to suit her perfectly.

* * * * * * * * * *

Monday morning Julie drove to her new office, a wood-shingled old house converted to a small realty firm. Since she was new and part-time, she was given a desk in a room in the back. This was fine with her. She had views in the other parts of her life--at home and in the car. She'd probably be able to work a little better without the distractions of the river or the ocean.

She spent the morning settling in after she was introduced to the other five agents, three of whom also worked part-time. This seemed to be a pretty low-pressure office, not at all like the high-powered one she'd left downtown. What a great way to start easing into retirement. She was given the calendar for the next few weeks showing when she was scheduled to work the "up desk," the time she sat at the front desk, greeted clients, and took calls from prospective buyers and sellers. Those clients without an agent would be hers, the perk of working the "up desk." Other than that, she was free to come in as she felt she needed to with the goal of averaging at least twenty hours of work a week, including showing homes, visiting listings, sitting open houses, and working the "up desk."

Since she was working for the company she'd been with in the city, the computer system was the same. She plugged in her laptop, hung her certificate on the wall, organized her desk, made a list of supplies she needed, and ordered her business cards. By noon she was ready to leave for the day and eager to get home. It was a perfect day to be outdoors, and she thought she'd do a little work in her garden.

When she got home, however, her plans changed. Inside her picket fence she found the cutest little scrawny cat crying piteously. As she reached down, it moved away from her as if frightened. She got down on her knees and called softly to it holding out her hand but trying not to scare it. It finally moved forward, very slowly. She reached for its little gray body and picked it up.

She'd wanted a cat for years, but Ted wouldn't hear of it. "Too messy," he'd said. "Cat fur all over everything. Too much trouble. And cat litter! Yuk."

But Ted didn't live here--she could have a cat again. She held the scared animal in her arms and carried her inside. Obviously this was not someone's pet, although she would check with the lost and found at the humane society to be sure. But it looked like this cat needed a home.

Sheba, she thought. *I'll name her Sheba.* Sheba had been her childhood cat whom she'd loved dearly. Good memories of a cat who'd allowed her to dress it in doll clothes, rode in her bicycle basket, and cuddled with her on her bed. Sheba lived a long life of almost twenty years. That was a good omen for this kitty.

She opened the fridge, put the frightened cat down, and poured a little milk in a bowl for her. After a moment's hesitation, Sheba lapped it up hungrily. Julie went to the yellow pages looking for a pet store and a vet. She also called the humane society. They had no record of anyone looking for this cat, so she made a late afternoon appointment for the next day at the vet's. Then she drove to the pet store located on the main highway about a mile away and bought a litter box, litter, food, dishes, and toys.

When she got home, Sheba was hiding under the bed but quickly came out when she heard the clatter of the can and can opener. So, at one time she'd lived in a home and been fed, Julie thought as she put the food and water dishes in the laundry room. While Sheba ate, she set up the litter box as well. Sheba investigated it when she was through eating and seemed to know its purpose with no problems.

Life was getting better. She had a home, a new part-time job, some friends, and a furry companion. She checked her answering machine. The blinking light showed her a message. One call. From Bill. Was she ready to even think about getting involved with another man? Was this what she wanted or needed at this point in her life? She was just beginning to enjoy her life by herself. *Stop being silly,* she told herself. *A phone call does not mean a commitment. It means a nice man wants to be your friend.*

His message was brief, asking her to give him a call when she got in.

As she dialed his number, she had doubts but decided not to be a coward.

He answered, obviously recognizing her number, "Hi Julie. How are you?"

"Fine," she responded. "I've just been adopted by a cat," and she told him about Sheba.

"Cats are good company," he said. "I've had them in the past myself. Anyway, I know you weren't sure you wanted to surf. But how about kayaking? You mentioned loving to float on the water. Good weather's projected for tomorrow. I've got a spare. Would you like to go?"

"Kayaking? I've only kayaked a few times in my younger years, but it does sound like fun, if you don't mind a novice."

"Not at all. Nothing to it. It's calm out on the lake."

"Well, sure then," Julie answered, and he said he'd pick her up at nine in the morning.

Sheba came in and groomed herself. She looked much happier than the mewing baby who'd been in the yard. Soon she was exploring the house, checking out each piece of furniture from the top to the bottom. Then she found the ball Julie had purchased and began batting it around. Sheba was going to be entertaining as well as good company.

Chapter Four

Julie did not sleep in Tuesday morning. She got up early, debated what to wear, and wondered if she should bring some food along. Kayaking sounded like it might be a lot of work, but Bill had mentioned floating on the water. She had a feeling he was much more athletic than she when it came to the outdoors.

She finally dressed in sandals, cropped pants, and a long-sleeved shirt, put sunscreen all over her face and neck, and made sure she had her sunglasses and a hat. Then, realizing she still had time, she raided the fridge and cupboards for some cheese and crackers, cookies, and apples, and filled two bottles with water.

The doorbell rang. Bill was there.

He smiled when she answered the door, and she knew it would be a good day. He was so warm and friendly--his face crinkled when he smiled.

In a few minutes time they were off in his pickup with the kayaks stashed in the back. A myriad of lakes surrounded the town, and he found one in the dunes that wasn't too large and didn't allow motor vehicles of any kind. Rolling dunes and pines surrounded the sparkling lake which was dotted by a few other colorful kayaks--they looked like the primary colors in a Crayola box.

Once they were in the water, she easily paddled her blue boat around the lake. Then they decided to explore a finger heading toward the ocean. It was so serene and incredibly beautiful. She felt like she was on vacation and laughed to herself. She actually lived here now.

Bill was easy to be with, showing her how to paddle efficiently. They moved slowly through the water, having quiet conversation as they drifted watching the world around them. He pointed out several osprey nests, a great blue heron, and further down the finger, they watched enthralled as a family of river otters entertained them. They put ashore at a campground and enjoyed the snacks Julie had brought, while sitting at a picnic table.

"Julie, I think you're taking to this like a natural," Bill said.

"I was thinking the same thing," she responded. "I think I'd like to get a kayak of my own. This is the most peaceful way to be outdoors. I've enjoyed it so much. Do you know where I could get a kayak? Are there many different kinds? What should I look for?"

"Hold on," he answered. "Why don't you just borrow mine for a few weeks, and then I can help you look for one. I'm sure this one will fit on the rack of your SUV, or maybe we can even squeeze it inside. We can try fitting it in your car when we get back to your house. You can borrow the life jacket as well. Lots of us have kayaks, so you can probably find someone to go with any day you want."

"Wow. Are you sure you don't mind? I'll take care of it. I haven't done anything I've enjoyed so much in ages."

"No problem. And perhaps we can go out again together," he said.

"That would be great," she answered. *Really great*, she thought.

They had a leisurely paddle back up the lake and loaded the kayaks into his truck. He dropped her off with the blue kayak and helped her slip it into the back of her Lexus where it fit perfectly with the rear seats folded down and the front passenger seat all the way back. He said he'd call in a couple of days and maybe they could kayak again on a different lake.

What a great way to spend a morning, she thought, as she showered, dressed in sweats, and then headed for the grocery store.

After she returned home and put away her groceries, she noticed her answering machine was blinking. But glancing at the clock, she realized that she needed to get Sheba to her vet appointment. The answering machine would have to wait.

The vet said that Sheba was probably about a year old, had been spayed, but should be vaccinated as a precaution. Julie agreed and was relieved to know that Sheba was in good health. The vet remarked that cats were dropped off at the beach fairly regularly, so probably no one was looking for her.

"In these economic times," he said, "more and more people are discovering they can't afford to keep their pets. Unfortunately, they drop them off thinking they will be rescued by someone. Often house pets starve to death or become victims of predators. In this case, Sheba was lucky."

Sheba was glad to get home, and Julie busied herself fixing both of them dinner. It had been a fun but exhausting day. She turned on the TV and tuned out.

* * * * * * * * * *

At about nine, while dozing in front of the television, Julie was awakened by the phone. She couldn't imagine who could be calling at that time of night, but then remembered the blinking answering machine that she'd forgotten to check when she and Sheba came back from the vet's. She fumbled for the receiver on the end table.

"Hello," she said.

"Julie, is that you?" a man's voice asked.

She shook her head and blinked her eyes.

"Why didn't you call me back?" he demanded.

She sat up, suddenly realizing it was Ted.

"Ted, what's the matter?"

"It's Tina. She's been murdered," he sobbed.

"Murdered? That's terrible. What happened?"

"Worst of all," he continued. "The police are questioning me, and I'm afraid they're going to arrest me. I need your help."

Julie was shocked but still couldn't get over the fact that Ted had just said that possibly being arrested was worse than Tina's death. So like Ted to put himself first.

"What do you need from me?" she asked, not wanting to get involved, but they had been married for twenty years, and, in fact, legally they still were. The divorce wasn't final yet.

"No one believes me," he said. "Neighbors heard us fighting this afternoon. I went out for a walk, and when I came back, she'd been killed with a kitchen knife. There was blood everywhere. It was awful. Everyone thinks I did it. I can't stand it here. I'm afraid they'll lock me up. I need to get out. I called you right after I called the police. You didn't answer or call back. They just now let me call you again. Can you help me?"

"Slow down, Ted. I'm taking this all in. Have you phoned your attorney?"

"Don's not answering. I have no idea who else to call. I've got to get out of here. You've no idea how horrible it is. I don't think they believe me. Please help me!"

"Oh, my god. Let me see. I'll try Don again for you. Did you try his home number?"

"No, I didn't have it on my cell, and it's not listed," he replied.

"Okay, let me start there. Give me the number where you can be reached."

He gave her the station's number and begged, "Please hurry."

As she hung up, she paused for a moment and almost laughed. No, she could not imagine fastidious Ted in jail, if it came to that.

She looked up Don and Judy Anderson's home number in her address book and called.

"Judy, this is Julie Maxwell," she said as the phone was answered.

"Yes?" Judy replied, clearly not pleased with a late evening call.

"Sorry to bother you, but I need to talk to Don about a legal matter. It's really important. Please."

"O.K., Julie. Let me go get him. He's in his office working."

Don came to the phone. "Hi, Julie. What's so important that it can't wait until morning?"

"It's Ted," she said. "Tina's been murdered, and he's being questioned. He thinks he might be arrested. He's been trying to reach you but didn't have your home number. Apparently your work cell wasn't ringing, or something."

"No, I left my mobile at work. Now, what's this about Ted?"

After she told him what little she knew, he said he'd drive down to the station immediately and asked whether she could meet him there.

Julie groaned, saying, "Yeah, I'll drive into the city."

"Drive into the city? Where are you living?"

"The beach," she replied. "It'll take about an hour."

"That should be about right," he said. "I'll have plenty to do first. See you there."

She hung up and decided she'd better throw on some slacks and a sweater; sweats seemed a little too casual for the city. As she opened the garage door, she realized the kayak was still in the car. She pulled it out and stowed it in the garage. If he were released, Ted would need to ride in the passenger seat back to his condo.

Life had been so peaceful for the past few weeks. Leave it to Ted to screw things up. But he was in a real predicament, she realized, as she thought about the fact that Tina had been murdered. Could Ted have done it? She really didn't think so, but who could have come into the condo while he was out? And why?

Chapter Five

It was a pretty drive through the mountains into the city where the bright lights were almost a shock to her after the quiet darkness of the beach. With her GPS she located the police station, finally found parking, and entered. After checking in, she took a seat. God, she wished she'd thought to bring a book. She'd never even been in a police station before. However, soon she saw that it was an interesting place to people watch--apparent hookers, drug dealers, and who knew who else were coming in and out. For some it appeared to be a fairly routine part of their lives.

She saw Don approaching from across the room. He was dressed in his lawyer's suit and vest looking quite the professional. She was glad she'd not worn her sweats.

"Julie, so good of you to come. We don't need to worry about arrest or bail as Ted's currently only considered a person of interest. He should be out soon."

They sat down next to each other and waited for Ted to be released, chatting about her move.

Don gestured. "There he is." Then he stood, waved his arm, and said, "Hey Ted, over here."

Julie barely recognized the man who looked old and dazed as he entered the lobby. It was Ted, but a Ted she'd never seen before. His clothes were wrinkled, he had a five o'clock shadow or more on his jaw adding to the unkempt look, and his posture, usually strong and tall, reflected his decline in his sloping shoulders. As he grew closer, she saw that even the emerald eyes appeared to have lost some of their brilliance. Amazing what an afternoon and evening being questioned by the police could do to a man. *And finding Tina's body*, she reminded herself.

"Julie, thank you for coming and locating Don," Ted said.

She nodded, and then Ted turned to Don saying, "Don't know what I would have done without your help, buddy."

Don shook his hand and said, "Since it's nearing midnight, I'd better get home. And so should you. You look like you could use some sleep."

Ted agreed. "Yes, it's been a day I hope I never have to live through again."

Don added, "Good night, then. Ted, call me in the morning, and we'll work on what happens next." He turned to Julie. "Good night, and thanks for driving in."

"Good night, Don, and thank you," she answered.

Ted looked at Julie. "It was awful in there," he said. " By the way, I'm going to need to spend the night with you. They won't let me back into the crime scene."

The crime scene--his condo. She should've thought of that.

"I don't think that's a good idea, Ted. It's an hour away at the beach. How about I check you into a hotel instead?"

Ted begged. "Julie, please let me stay with you. I can't bear to be alone. You've no idea what it was like finding Tina's bloody body. It was horrible. Please."

Julie gave in. What else could she do? She could see that he was a mental mess as well as a physical one.

"You won't like my house," she said. "It's an old cottage, not your taste at all. And it's damp at the beach, just as you warned me. Are you sure you wouldn't be happier in a nice hotel?"

Ted shook his head and said he'd given her address and phone number to the police as his temporary residence. As they walked to her car, she was bothered by his assumption that he could just stay with her. *It can't be for long,* she thought, while she drove back over the mountains to the beach. Ted said little on the ride back.

He still seemed in shock when she pulled into the garage and led him into the house. Sheba ran to greet her, then backed off when she saw Ted. He didn't even notice the cat. In fact, he hardly took notice of the house.

"Would you like a drink and a bite to eat?" she asked.

He nodded as he slumped on the living room sofa, and said, "That would be nice. Whatever you have will be fine."

Julie fixed a plate with some olives, cheese, crackers, and fruit and poured them each a scotch. Still in shock, he ate but said very little.

When she led him to the guest bedroom, showed him the bathroom, and put out towels, he seemed very passive, just saying, "Thank you, Julie. I don't know what I'd do without you."

After he was settled in, she went upstairs to the crow's nest, finishing her scotch as she gazed at the sea. Sheba climbed up the stairs and hopped onto the couch next to her. As she petted her cat, she thought, *My life is going to change*. And not in the direction she'd been anticipating. Ted was part of it again whether she liked it or not.

She went down the stairs and climbed into her bed, knowing she would sleep restlessly, if at all.

Julie finally did get to sleep about 4:30. When she awoke to the sound of someone grinding coffee beans in her kitchen, she was startled. Then she remembered. Ted. Looking at the clock, she yawned. It was only seven. Although she didn't want to get up so early, she decided she'd better. The sooner she got up, perhaps the sooner she could get Ted back to the city.

After she'd showered and dressed, she came down the stairs. Ted was sitting at the counter drinking coffee and looking at the newspaper headlines.

"Well, I always wanted to be front page news," he said. "Only I wanted to be noticed for my decorating, not as the prime suspect in a murder case."

Julie glanced over his shoulder. "Renowned Local Designer Suspected of Grisly Murder. " No, that wasn't the kind of fame that anybody would want.

"I'm sorry, Ted. I'm sure you need to get back to the city. How soon do you want to go?"

"The city? I'm through with that place. I don't want to be hounded by reporters, asked a million questions. I just want to stay here where it's peaceful for awhile."

She shook her head. "This isn't going to work. I'm happy to help out, but I can't have you staying here. I have my own life now."

"Would you really just throw me to the wolves? Well, I guess I do deserve it, though you've always been a better person than me. Where's your compassion? I'm being considered a suspect in a murder I didn't commit. I need support. I need someone to take care of me."

There's the rub, she thought. Tina's dead, and he has no one to take care of him and his needs. So, as far as he was concerned, she was back in the picture.

Julie fixed their breakfast while Ted talked on the phone with Don. Ted said little while he ate his eggs and toast. He did thank her, but that was it. He was obviously preoccupied.

After doing the dishes, she went into the living room where he was slouched on the sofa.

"I need to get some clothes," he said. "Don told me I can't get back into the condo for at least another day. Is there anyplace out here where I can pick up a few things?"

She laughed as she told him, "Only Freddy's." She was sure he'd never been in a Fred Meyers in his life. But it would have to do.

When they returned to her cottage, he was shaking his head. "I never knew that you could buy so many things in a grocery department store," he said. "I think I'll go shower and put some clean clothes on."

As he headed off to the shower, Julie took the opportunity to read the complete newspaper article. Ted did look like the prime suspect. Oh god, her name was in the article as well--she was the estranged wife. Apparently there were no prints on the knife, and no one had seen or heard anything after Ted said he'd left for his walk. He was in deep shit, and Julie truly believed he didn't do it. He might be an arrogant bastard, but she didn't think he could kill someone, not unless that person threatened him in some way. Could Tina have threatened him? How?

Perhaps she'd better do what she could to help him out, or she'd continue to be stuck with him. She doubted he'd have any friends showing up to help. His friends were of the vanity variety-- the type he liked to show off to impress others, and vice versa. They wouldn't want to get their images tarnished. He was alone, except for her, and previously Tina. But Tina was no help now.

After Ted took off for a beach walk, she watched him hunker into the wind. He looked like a lost soul. He probably always had been underneath the veneer.

She decided she'd better call the office and let them know she probably wouldn't be in regularly for a while. Roger, the office broker, had seen the article in the paper and understood. He said he'd get others to cover and asked her to check in daily by phone. She agreed to do so.

Just as she hung up, the phone rang. It was Eleanor.

"Dear, how are you? I just saw it in the paper. I had no idea you were married to *the* Ted Larson--the decorator for the rich and famous. I do read the "Lifestyle" section of the city paper, you know. Anything I can do to help?"

"Well, it's awkward," Julie replied. "Ted's staying with me currently. I might need some escape time. Can I come over if I do?"

"Sure, what are friends for," Eleanor said. "Come over whenever you want."

Julie thought she might be needing that break soon as Ted came into the living room. He flopped on the couch and said, "Hey, Julie. As a thank you for your hospitality, I'll decorate this dump for you--no charge."

This dump! Julie was steamed. "Ted, do not refer to my home as a dump. It suits my tastes just the way it is. IF I decide to decorate, I'll do it myself, my way. Please understand I'm only helping you out because you were, legally are, my husband. But do not try to change me or my house. Understood?"

Ted looked confused. "I can't believe you're upset about an offer for free decorating. But sure, I didn't mean to offend you. If you like this . . ." His voice trailed off as if he couldn't believe it.

"Now," Julie said. "Let's get busy. What are we going to do to prove you're innocent?"

"Where do we even begin?" Ted asked piteously.

The doorbell saved Julie from answering him. She hoped the reporters hadn't discovered Ted was hidden away here, but they had. They were clamoring for Ted, who finally came out and said, "I didn't do it. No further comment."

Julie pulled him back in and went out to the group saying, "If you don't get off my property, I'm calling the sheriff. Please leave right now." And she marched back inside, peering though the window to observe them exiting her yard and driveway, clustering in the street beyond.

Chapter Six

As she joined Ted back in the living room, the doorbell rang again. Julie pulled back her shoulders, stood up straight, marched to the door, and was prepared to yell at the reporters again. However, when she opened the door, she saw Bill standing there, his blue eyes staring into hers with concern.

"Bill, what the hell are you doing here?" she asked. "Come to see the circus? Did the reporters let you through?"

Bill didn't look a bit ruffled. "No problem," he said, handing her a card. "I came to offer my services."

"Your services?" she asked. She glanced at the card. "Detective agency? That's the business you run?"

"Sure do. Part-time for cases that interest me. I usually choose my own clients rather than the other way around. Would you and your husband be interested in discussing his case with me?"

"Ex-husband," Julie clarified. "Or almost ex, when the divorce is final."

Ted stood up as they entered the living room.

"Ted," she said. "This is my neighbor and friend, William Smythe, Private Detective, known as Bill. He's offering to help you with your case. What do you think?"

Ted looked suspiciously from Julie to Bill. "How do you two know each other? What's going on between you two?"

Julie answered, "Ted, he's a friend. He's offering to help. I think we could use a few friends right now, don't you?"

Ted hesitated, studying Bill's face, then slowly relaxed. "I'm sorry," he said at last. "Please sit down. Julie, why don't you make some coffee while I chat with Bill?"

Damn, he was making her feel like his personal servant again. However, at least he was willing to talk with Bill. Entrepreneur, Bill had told her. She'd thought import-export or something exotic like that. But a P.I.? How interesting.

As Julie brought in the tray with the coffee, cups, sugar, creamer, and some banana nut bread she had in the fridge, Ted was telling Bill about Tina. Bill had a ton of questions. It was amazing how little Ted knew about her. They'd been together, professionally and then personally, for about three years, yet he really didn't know much about her, especially her past.

Tina's ex-husband, Reggie Denali, still lived in the city and remained quite angry about Tina's wanting a divorce. Apparently Tina had told him about Ted about five months ago, shortly before Julie learned that Tina was in the picture. The ex could be a likely candidate. As Bill asked about Tina, it was apparent that Ted had no idea who her friends were that she met with for coffee or anything about the art class she was taking. It occurred to Julie that he probably knew just as little about her even though they'd been married for twenty years. Life was always about him.

Well now it was about him in a big way.

"What do you think her husband does for a living?" Bill asked Ted.

"She said he was in finance, private deals. She said she didn't understand what he did, but he kept her in nice clothes, a fancy car, and they lived in a great condo. It was hard for her to decide to divorce him because he took such good care of her. However, she fell in love with me during the time we worked together and loved being a part of the design scene. When she told him she was leaving, he threatened her. But she wasn't scared. Said he was all talk. Maybe he wasn't."

"Okay, Ted," Bill said. "When you can get back into the condo, see what you can find in her personal stuff. The police will have confiscated some evidence--her calendar, cell phone, things like that. But see if you can find anything else. I suggest you go to your office today and look through all her things there since she was your assistant. The police might not've had a chance to do that. Can you leave now?"

When Ted looked at her, Julie nodded. "Sure, Ted. I'll take you to town." She turned to Bill and asked, "Anything else we should do while we're there?"

"Grab a picture of her, if you can, so that I can show it around to local coffee shops to see if anyone remembers her meeting friends there. Also, try to see if you can find out where she was taking art classes--maybe she had some brochures or something. I'll do some background on her ex-husband. Reggie? Right?"

Ted nodded. "Yeah, Reginaldo Denali is his real name. This guy is a bruiser, works out a lot. So did Tina though. Great body," he said, looking apologetically at Julie.

"What gym?" Bill asked. "Any chance they still worked out at the same place?"

"Yeah, they probably did. Just down the street from my studio and office. Forget the name, but a block away. I went there once or twice with Tina. Too professional for me--uh, Jake's Powerhouse, I think that's the name. Something like that. Not a typical spa, that's for sure," Ted added.

"Well, I'll see you tonight or tomorrow. You guys get into the office and studio, if you can, and see what you can rescue. Since it's not the crime scene, you may beat the cops there."

Twenty minutes later, Ted and Julie were headed back into the city. *Sorry I ever wanted to be Nancy Drew,* Julie thought as she wound through the mountains. Nancy Drew was a much younger woman, a girl really, not a middle-aged woman who was semi-retired living at the beach. *I'm too old to enjoy playing detective,* Julie thought.

Ted fiddled with the car radio, pulling out the Pink Martini CD she'd been listening to.

"Ted, quit that. We can't get much reception here. Please put the CD back in." Hell, if she was going to have to do this, at least she could listen to music she liked. Surprisingly, he complied without complaint.

As they pulled into the office and studio parking lot, there didn't appear to be any police activity. "Maybe we did beat the cops here," Ted said.

Julie nodded. "Let's just get in and see what we can find."

They took the elevator to the third floor. Ted's office and studio took up the whole floor, almost a block in size. Part of it was his showroom; the back was reserved for custom upholsterers, art collections, decor items, and his offices. They went directly into Tina's office.

"Wow, we're in luck," Ted said. "Here's her i-phone. It has her calendar, tons of apps, and a directory of all her phone numbers. Put it in your bag. I'm sure Bill will be able to use it."

Julie put the phone in her bag and opened the cupboards above the file cabinets behind the desk. As she shuffled through them, she found nothing but office supplies. She moved down to the filing cabinets while Ted continued to paw through the desk drawers. They were both startled by a huge man blocking the doorway. He looked like someone who should be named Bruno.

"Hey, what're you doing here?" Ted asked, as the man pushed him down on the floor by the desk. Bruno stood over him waving a tattooed hand with a gun in it.

"I want what's mine," he said.

"What's that?" Julie asked. She sat down in the desk chair, her knees shaking.

"She's got some of my stuff, and I want it. Where is it?"

"We can't help you if we don't know what it is?" Julie said, standing up. "Tell us what it is, and we'll try to help."

"Shuddup and sit down, bitch," he said.

Julie complied. The man stepped around her, banged open the cabinets, and took out a box the size that would hold dozens of manilla folders. Hoisting the box in his left hand, he motioned to them with the gun in his right, saying, "Not a word to the cops. Understand? Or both of you's dead. I'm not kidding." And he waved the gun at them.

They both nodded. Ted said, "As far as we're concerned, you were never here."

"Right, asshole," the man said, and left.

Julie was sure her heart would never regain its regular slower beat. Ted looked like a whipped puppy.

When she caught her breath, Julie picked up the phone and said, "We've got to call the police."

Ted jumped to his feet, pulling the phone out of her hand. "Are you crazy? Didn't you hear that man? No way or we're dead meat."

"Ted, this might be what you're looking for. He might hold the key to Tina's murder. Don't you want the murderer found? It'll get you off the hook."

"Not at the cost of my own life, thank you. We aren't telling anyone. Clear!" he ordered.

"Well at least we'll tell Bill. Can you describe him? I think I can. Huge, bald, a tattoo of something evil looking on his right arm. Did you see it? Apparently that wasn't Tina's ex?"

"No, but it could've been one of his buddies. The tattoo wasn't totally recognizable to me, especially since the gun was in that hand and he kept waving it--maybe a dragon or a big snake. Are you sure we should tell Bill? What do you really know about him? Can we trust him?"

"Think about it, Ted. Who else are we going to turn to for help? Bill's a god-send. This is the first clue we've had--someone who said Tina had something of his. Maybe that was the reason. Maybe he thought it was at your condo, and that's why he showed up there and killed her. Maybe . . ."

"If he's the killer, why didn't he kill us, too?"

"Maybe," Julie answered, thinking aloud, "maybe he thought three murders would be too messy, plus you're the current prime suspect. If he kills you, the police start looking for someone else."

"Okay, okay. We tell Bill. But not the police. I'm through looking. Let's get the hell out of here."

They left the parking lot and were down the street just before an unmarked police car turned the corner. Probably there to secure the premises and Tina's office. Well, too late. At least they had the phone.

Chapter Seven

Ted was still visibly shaken as Julie drove back to the beach. He didn't say anything, just curled up in the passenger seat while she hummed along with Pink Martini wondering what was in that box and what else Tina might have had. Could she have been involved in drugs, some kind of blackmail, some financial scheme? Maybe they'd know more when they learned what Bill had found out about her background.

As they pulled into Julie's driveway, Bill's pickup came in right behind them. Good timing, Julie thought.

"Did you find anything?" Bill asked.

"Tell you inside," Julie said, looking around. She would hate for Bruno to show up here, but it didn't look like they'd been followed as she drove home, and she didn't see anything unusual on her street.

When they were settled in the living room, Ted pulled Tina's i-phone out of Julie's bag and handed it to Bill.

"Good find," Bill said. "I'll take it home and go over all the calls made and received, all the apps, the calendar, and phone directory. This may provide some good info for us."

"What have you found out?" Julie asked.

"Well, Tina's an interesting case. She appears to have no family. Did she ever mention family, Ted?"

"No, not really. She knew I was an orphan, raised in foster homes, and she sounded like she was, too. We never really talked about it. We seemed pretty much alike in regards to our pasts. Not something either of us really wanted to think about, much less discuss."

"Well, her past is a bit different. She didn't exist until shortly before she met you. There's no record of her birth, certainly not as Tina Randall, which you said was her name when she married. Her life seemed to begin with her wedding certificate. Apparently she didn't have a social security card until then either, which is highly unusual, unless she changed her identity. No teenage driver's license, no school records that we can find at the art institute in New York. It's like she was invented as an adult."

"I don't have any information to help you," Ted answered. "When she came to work for me, she was already married, had a social security card in that name, said she'd been to art school back east, like I told you. I never checked her references. She seemed perfect for the job."

"What does that mean, she doesn't have a past?" Julie asked.

"I'm not sure. Could be that she was into some illegal activity and had to have a new identity."

Julie said, "Bill, something happened in town. We had a visitor with a gun in the office."

She described the guy she'd named Bruno and explained what he'd taken. "Do you think he was looking for it at the condo and killed Tina when she wouldn't tell him where it was?"

"Could be," Bill said. "Or she told him it was at the office, and he killed her anyway so she wouldn't squeal on him. I wonder if we should get a security detail here. He, or his boss, might have second thoughts about your seeing him, and he might come looking for you two."

Julie shivered at the thought of seeing Bruno again.

"Don't you think he would have taken us out there if he intended to?" Ted asked. "He told us not to go to the police, and we haven't."

"He may not have wanted murder victims found in Tina's office. Maybe he's happier that it looks like you're going to take the rap for murder. Who knows? I wish I knew what was in that box. What size was it?"

Julie answered, "It looked like a box that eight by ten manilla folders come in. It didn't appear particularly heavy as he picked it up, surely no heavier than folders would be. I saw it on the shelf, but I wouldn't have even opened it because it was in a cabinet with other supplies. He obviously knew what he was looking for."

"We seem to have more questions than answers," Bill said. "Let me look over the phone and get back to you later today or tomorrow."

"Thanks, Bill. We really appreciate your help," Julie said, as they walked him to the door.

* * * * * * * * *

After Julie and Ted returned home from dinner at an Italian cafe downtown, she told him she needed some alone time.

"Fix yourself a drink, some coffee, whatever. The living room is yours. Read, watch TV. I'm going upstairs."

"Hey, Julie. Thanks. You've done so much for me. I don't know what I'd do without you."

"Sure, Ted," she said. "Good night."

She stopped by her bedroom, threw on some pajamas, and headed to the crow's nest. After she lit the fireplace, she stretched out on the couch and listened to the surf. *Ted had a valid point,* she mused. *Why do I trust Bill?* As she thought it over, she realized that he'd certainly shown up quickly after the news broke. He'd handed her a business card, and she took him at face value. How naive was that? And now he had Tina's phone. They hadn't really even looked at it. Tomorrow she'd do a bit of investigation on her own. Make sure Mr. William Smythe was really who he said he was.

Sheba climbed up on her lap. "Silly kitty," she said, stroking her fur. "What's happening to me? Why am I unsure about Bill?"

As thoughts of conspiracies and Bill, Tina, and Bruno swirled through her mind, she fell into a restless sleep on the couch. At midnight, she woke up and went downstairs to her own room. The living room lights were on and the TV mumbled. Ted must still be up, she thought. He's probably having trouble sleeping.

She crawled into her bed with plans to investigate Bill on the Internet. She realized that she hadn't really convinced herself that he could be trusted. He'd been just a little too handy.

The sun was shining brightly when she woke up the next morning, and Sheba was staring her in the face eager for her to awaken. She glanced at the clock. Nine a.m. Wow, she'd really slept in, and sweet Sheba hadn't bothered her, just sat there staring and waiting for movement.

"Good kitty," she said as she went into the bathroom to shower and get dressed.

Ted was drinking coffee when she came down to the kitchen. He was rumpled looking. He must've slept on the living room couch, if he slept at all.

"Rough night?" she asked.

He looked down at his wrinkled shirt and pants, rubbed his unshaven face, and nodded. "Jeez, I must look like hell," he said. "I'll go shower and dress." He carried his coffee up the stairs with him.

In the light of morning, Julie's fears about Bill from the previous night seemed a little overblown. After all, she did meet him through friends, and he was a neighbor. However, she thought, it wouldn't hurt to check. Then she could have complete confidence in him.

She decided to give Eleanor and Jenn calls to see how much they knew about their friend Bill. Then she would do an ID search on the computer and see what turned up.

She fixed some toast, drank her coffee, and then dialed Eleanor.

"Hey, Eleanor," she said. "Good morning. Julie here. Just a couple of questions. What can you tell me about Bill?"

"Good morning," Eleanor replied. "So, you do like him. I thought so. You two look cute together. Is your ex-husband still there? Doesn't that make it confusing?"

"Kind of," Julie responded. Why not let her think she was asking questions because she was interested in Bill romantically? "What does he do for a living? Has he ever been married?"

"Let's see," Eleanor answered. "He runs some kind of business part-time. He must do well because he has a great house, surfs all over the world. He's never mentioned marriage, but he never talks about the women he sees either. Actually, for as personable as he is, he's rather tight-lipped."

Well, she thought, hanging up. Interesting. Eleanor had known Bill for three years, since he moved to the beach, and knew no more about him than she did. She thought he owned some kind of a business, the old "entrepreneur" thing again, and that he must be successful since he surfs all over the world. As far as she knew, there apparently was no wife, or serious girlfriend, past or present. That's odd in a man in his fifties, she thought. Eleanor had suggested that Julie call Phil and Jon since they surfed with Bill on a regular basis.

Julie decided that rather than call, she'd talk to them in person. They might share more willingly, both of them, face-to-face rather than one at a time on the phone.

Chapter Eight

Julie laced up her tennies and walked across the street to Jon and Phil's home. Theirs was a more modern beach home, kind of mid-century style. Phil was in the garden when she came up the walkway. He wore a straw gardening hat that covered his blond hair. He probably needed to wear it since he freckled easily and most likely burned quickly. He was kneeling with a weeder in his hand and looked up as she approached.

"Hi neighbor," he said, standing up and smiling at Julie. "What brings you to our abode?"

"Oh, just wanted to say hi, and actually I have something I'd like to talk to you both about, if Jon's home."

"Sure, come on in. I could use a break. Jon's cleaning up the breakfast dishes."

Phil led her upstairs to the kitchen and living room. " Jon, look who's come to visit," Phil said, and then asked her, "Would you like some coffee?"

As Julie nodded yes to the coffee, Jon peeked out from the kitchen wearing an apron over his tee shirt and shorts. He and Phil were about the same height, five foot nine or so, a little taller than she was.

"Why hi, Julie," he said, his balding head shining while his graying goatee moved with his generous smile. "What can we do for you?"

"Well, I wanted to take you up on your offer to see your house, and I have a few questions for you, if you don't mind."

"Now, I'm really curious," he answered. "But first, the drinks."

Jon brought the coffee out and settled on the couch next to her. Phil sat across from her on the other side of the coffee table.

As she sipped her coffee, Julie decided to act like she was just nosy about Bill because they'd gone out together.

"You probably know I went kayaking with Bill," she said. "I realize that I know nothing about him. Is he single?"

Jon and Phil looked at one another.

"I guess so," Phil finally said. "He's never talked about anybody, seems to have a lot of female friends, and hasn't hit on either one of us, so I don't think he's gay."

Jon agreed. "I believe he's straight, if that helps. But I don't know if he's ever been married. He doesn't talk much about his private life."

"What does he do for a living?" Julie asked.

"Gee, I think he owns some kind of business," Phil said. "Maybe something to do with importing or investments. He's never really told us."

Jon added, "He obviously makes good money. Not like us teachers who have to count pennies. And he certainly has lots of free time. Our only free time is the summer and weekends."

"Come to think of it, Jon," Phil said. "We really don't know what he does. We've talked about it and tried to pin him down a bit, but he just changes the subject. Face it, we mostly know him as a fellow surfer. Are you serious about him? Do you want us to see if we can learn anything about past women, etc.?"

"Well, if you can do it subtly. I've been hurt before, as you've probably read in the paper, and I want to be really careful who comes into my life now." This was the perfect excuse, she thought, because they both nodded.

"Yeah, we didn't want to bring it up," Jon said. "Pretty terrible about your ex-husband. Eleanor says he's staying with you. That must be difficult."

"Oh, you don't know how difficult," she replied.

They chatted about her ex, and then Jon offered to show her around the house. It was situated at the top of the dunes directly across the street from her house, so it was even higher than hers. They'd walked up the stairs to the living room and kitchen area when she'd first come in. This floor had an almost total glass west wall which afforded an incredible view of the beach, blocked a little by her crow's nest. As she neared the window, she realized that they could look down to her driveway and front door. Obviously, they were aware that Ted was there. They could see her comings and goings. Their bedroom was on the lower level where the ocean view didn't exist but instead looked out on the beautifully kept gardens. The other room, tucked behind the garage, was an efficient office, with just one small window.

"We're surfing with Bill this afternoon," Phil said at the door. "He called about an hour ago and said the waves are great down south. We'll see what we can find out and get back to you."

"Yeah, and good luck getting your husband out of your life," Jon added. "Talk to you later today."

She thanked them and headed home.

When she walked in, she heard Ted on the phone. "Thanks, Don. I'll try to get to the condo today. Not sure where Julie's off to or what her plans are. Thanks. Bye."

He looked up and saw Julie. "That was Don," he said. "The cops are through at the crime scene, and I can get in to get some of my stuff and look through Tina's things. Don advised me to hire a specialty cleaning crew to clean up the blood and stuff. He gave me a number." He looked at her. "Did you have a good walk?"

Julie nodded. Then as she thought about the crime scene blood, she shuddered. "I'll take you to town, Ted. But I'm not going into the condo. I don't want to see the blood. Ugh." And she thought to herself, *I don't need the memories the condo brings back either.*

As Julie sat in her parked car in the condo garage waiting for Ted, she shivered. She hated parking garages, but the idea of the blood-spattered kitchen bothered her more. She checked to make sure the car doors were locked, and then she looked at the paper she'd brought along. Ted was no longer front-page news, but she found a small article stating that he was still the person of interest and that the investigation was continuing. So far he looked like not just the prime suspect, but the only one.

She wondered if she'd been too quick to let him off the hook. Could Tina have gotten violent and forced Ted to defend himself? This was all so confusing.

She pulled a notebook out of her purse and started a list:

> *(1) Who was Tina and why might Ted have been angry?*
>
> *(2) Who is Bill and what is his interest in helping?*
>
> *(3) Where did Bruno fit in and what was in that box?*

As the thoughts stirred in her head, her cell rang. It was the police department. They were trying to locate Ted, and he wasn't answering her home phone. She told them Ted was at his condo, and she was in the garage waiting for him. Ted was ordered to come down to the police department as soon as possible. The detectives had some new information. They also had to question her as his estranged wife.

Julie dialed Don. "Don, I think we need an attorney again. We're at the condo. Ted's upstairs. The cops just called and want him to come downtown. They have new information. My feeling is that it isn't good for Ted. And I need you, too. They also have to question me."

Don said he would meet them there in about a half hour. "Tell Ted not to say a word if he gets there before me. Better yet, arrive in forty-five minutes. That gives me plenty of time to get there first. And Julie, I can't really represent you and Ted both. However, I can be present while they question you, if that's okay with you."

Julie agreed and then hung up. She restlessly thumbed through the newspaper. Several more investment firms going under, missing money from a large insurance corporation, drugs, child sex rings . . . same old sad stuff.

When Ted finally came down, Julie looked at her watch and realized that if they left immediately, they would make it to the station when Don wanted them to arrive. Ted was unhappy with this change of plans.

"They can't make me come in." Then he asked, "Why should I go voluntarily?"

"Well, actually, they can make you go. They can come and arrest you. Don said it would be better if you came in on your own. We're not sure what this is about. They also want to question me."

"You?" he asked. "Why you?"

"Well, Ted, I am the aggrieved wife," she answered. Then noticing the suitcase he brought with him, she asked, "Hey, did you find anything?"

"No, just grabbed some of my clothes and things. Picked up a photo of Tina for Bill. Didn't see anything of Tina's that looked interesting."

She started the car and drove across town to the station. Don greeted them in the parking lot. "It's better if we go in together," he said.

They were met by a rumpled-looking detective who introduced himself as Detective John Gallagher. He reminded Julie of that TV detective who always had just one more question-- Columbo, that was his name. The major difference was this guy focused both his eyes on you, somewhat coldly, she thought. And he wore glasses.

Detective Gallagher turned to her. "You can wait here, Ma'am. There's a few magazines over there." He pointed to a small table. "We'll talk to you after we're through with him."

Ted looked at Don. "Can't she come, too?" he asked. "She knows everything that's going on. I'd like her there."

Don looked at the detective, who nodded and said, "Sure, if you don't care what she learns."

Julie followed them into the detective's cramped office where he pointed to several chairs and asked them to be seated. His desk looked about as messy as any desk she'd ever seen: five or six stacks of fat file folders, what looked like lists on yellow legal pads, and several half empty styrofoam cups. But he had no trouble pulling out the file he needed.

He opened the folder. Then, looking Ted straight in the eye, he asked, without preamble, "How did you feel about Tina's pregnancy?"

Julie felt her stomach lurch as she realized how much she'd wanted a child and how much Ted didn't. She eyed Ted cautiously.

"What do you mean, pregnant?" Ted asked. "She wasn't pregnant. She couldn't have been. I had a vasectomy years ago." He looked apologetically at Julie.

He'd never told her about a vasectomy. He really didn't want children. So what did this mean? Whose was it? Had the vasectomy failed? Did Ted know about the pregnancy? That could be motive to kill on his part.

Ted continued to deny that he'd known about the pregnancy and agreed to a DNA test to see if he was the father. He looked beat up. This was really bad for him.

"She was two months along. Didn't you notice anything?" Detective Gallagher badgered.

"Enough," Don interrupted. "Ted said he didn't know. He's agreed to a test. Can he go now?"

"After we do the test. But don't leave the area," he threatened Ted.

"I know," Ted replied. "I'm still at the beach at Julie's house."

God, she thought. *I wonder how much longer he'll need to stay.*

Gallagher returned Ted's cell phone that he'd confiscated the day of the murder, and then called an associate to come take Ted for his test.

After Ted left, Gallagher turned to her. "Do you want him in here?" he asked, pointing to Don. "It might be a conflict of interest."

"No, it's okay," she answered. "I want him to stay."

"Okay, we need to know your whereabouts the day of the murder."

"Yes, sir," Julie responded. "Well I spent the morning and early afternoon kayaking with a friend. Then when I got home, I showered, changed, and went grocery shopping. After that I took my cat to the vet for a four o'clock appointment. And, I live an hour away at the beach."

"Sounds as if you're in the clear. You wouldn't have had time to get into town and back again. Give me the name of your kayaking pal and the vet, please."

Julie complied, and she and Don left.

Chapter Nine

Ted was unusually quiet on the drive back to the beach, leaving Julie alone with her thoughts. She'd always thought that she'd be a mother. For the first few years of their marriage, she'd hoped that Ted would change his mind, especially as he became more successful. But if anything, he'd become more determined not to be a father. She'd always assumed it was due to his childhood, or perhaps his narcissism. Maybe he'd had the feeling that he couldn't totally trust her not to get pregnant, and he'd had the vasectomy then. Or maybe he'd started having affairs. Maybe Tina wasn't the first.

Dammit, there was so much she didn't really know about him. Could he have killed Tina because of the baby? Did he hate the idea of fatherhood that much? And, if it wasn't his, didn't that make it worse? Could he have killed her because she cheated on him?

As they walked in, she saw that the answering machine light was blinking away. Bill had called. So had Jon and Phil. She wasn't sure she was in the mood to talk to anybody but decided to get it over with.

"Ted, I've got a couple of calls to make," she called out. "I'm going upstairs to return them. Help yourself to whatever you need."

Sheba was sprawled out over the middle of the sofa in the crow's nest, so Julie made herself comfortable in the wing-back chair. Stretching her feet out on the ottoman, she decided to dial the guys first.

"Hi, this is Julie."

"Jon, here. Hi. We've got very little to report. Bill talked favorably about you, did not take our bait about former wives, etc. He hinted at unusual investments as his line of work. But even when Phil pretended that he had a small inheritance to invest, Bill didn't jump in. He just said that maybe they could get together later. No real information, I'm afraid."

"Well, thanks for trying," she said. "I really appreciate your help. That was very kind of you. See you soon." She hung up.

One down, one to go. She might as well get it over with, she thought, and rang Bill.

He answered on the first ring. "Why hi, Julie. Busy day? I have some info for you two. Mind if I come on over?"

She really didn't feel like entertaining either Bill or Ted, but the information might be valuable.

"Sure. Why don't you come on over for dinner. We're going to fix salmon and a salad, if you're interested. About six?"

"Sounds good to me. I'll bring some wine."

Julie got up, stretching her arms and legs, and then sat back in the chair thinking. Maybe Bill was an investment broker who also ran a detective agency. Maybe the investment business was a front for his detective agency. What the hell, maybe he was a spy. Who knew? And why couldn't she just let the police deal with it?

"Julie," Ted called. "Can you come down?"

Oh right, she thought. She had to do whatever she could to help the police solve this murder so that she could get Ted out of her house and her life.

"Coming, Ted," she answered. Sheba jumped off the sofa and followed her down the stairs.

"Hey. What's with your upstairs room? When can I see it?"

"Ted, I told you. That's my private space, which I need now more than ever. I really don't feel like showing it to anybody. Okay?"

"Okay, don't be so grumpy. Shall I start dinner?"

"That'd be great," she answered. "Bill's joining us. He said he had a little information."

Ted cooked, and she set the table. A little bit like old times. They really were a good pair when it came to entertaining. They fit back into a comfortable routine.

Ted and Bill were her first dinner guests in this house. She guessed she couldn't call Ted a guest as he was cooking dinner and temporarily living there. Anyway, it was fun to set a table. She just wished the dinner conversation could be about something other than murder. In fact, she'd insist upon it. No murder conversation until after dinner when they sat in the living room. Dinner would be a chance to get to know one another and maybe find out something more about Bill. She still hadn't had a chance to look him up on the Internet, but as secretive as he was with friends, she doubted that there'd be much there.

After Julie laid the ground rules of no murder business until after dinner, the three of them had enjoyed a nice evening. They'd had cocktails around the kitchen bar while Ted finished cooking, and then they'd sat down to a delicious salmon, perfect saffron rice, and a wonderful salad. Ted had even thawed and heated some dinner rolls. And the Viognier that Bill brought was delicious.

Conversation was light. Bill filled them in about surfing and the beach community but revealed little about himself. He asked questions that allowed Ted to talk about himself, something that Ted did quite well. He even offered to help Bill decorate his place. Bill nodded, as if interested.

After dinner, they settled into the living room with brandies. At last it was time to see what Bill had learned.

He'd checked the apps and not found anything too interesting. In checking her phone history, he found a couple of calls to an OB/GYN, to the gym, Jake's Powerhouse, and a number of calls to her ex-husband. There'd also been several calls to numbers that he was still investigating.

Her calendar showed an appointment with the OB/GYN, art class (although it didn't say where), and a dinner at the Cliff Inn two nights before the murder. Bill looked at Ted, who shook his head.

"I was working late that night," he said. "I assumed that she'd just gone home for dinner. I don't know who she might've met."

"Well, I'll check that in person. Did you get the photo I asked for so that I can take it with me?"

"Oh, sure," Ted responded. "I picked one up in the condo. I'll get it in a minute. What else?"

"Well, my staff did some background work. I have contacts with fingerprinting connections. We were able to get her prints from the DMV. Don't ask me how," he said, looking at their raised eyebrows. "Anyway, a national data base search is being done right now. I should have something by tomorrow. We're looking into the OB/GYN visit. Probably routine." But when he saw the expression on Julie's face, he asked, "What is it?"

"We know about that," Julie said. "It turns out Tina was pregnant."

"What?" Bill said, surprise on his face.

She and Ted told him what they'd learned and about the DNA test Ted had taken. She added, "We should know something tomorrow."

"Well," Bill said at last. "That certainly adds another dimension to the case, doesn't it? One of my associates is going to the gym tomorrow to see what we can learn about the guy you call Bruno and also find out who Tina hung around with while there. I think there may be a connection, but I'm not sure what it is yet. So, that takes care of business, I think."

"Not quite, Bill," Julie added. "The police may contact you to check on my alibi--to verify the fact that I was kayaking with you on the day of the murder."

"Sure, I figured at some point that would happen. But you didn't tell them I was working for Ted, did you? I don't want them putting a leash on my investigation."

"No, I didn't even think of that. Anyway, it's just the alibi that they're interested in. I guess a wronged wife could be a good suspect."

"Well, I can cover your morning," Bill said grinning. "Even if you'd had time to get into town after kayaking, you would have been hard-pressed to kill Tina and make it back to the vet's on time. I think you're in the clear."

But Ted was not. They quietly watched the summer sun set, late in the evening this far north, leaving traces of purple and orange on the water and wet sand, each of them apparently wrapped up in individual thoughts. Bill broke the silence, thanked them for dinner, and left.

"I'm relieved we have him helping us," Ted said, as he stood up and went into the kitchen to do dishes.

"Yeah," Julie agreed half-heartedly, wondering exactly what was in this for Bill. Oh, he'd charge Ted. They'd already discussed the fee, but what else?

Chapter Ten

Her crow's nest really was her refuge with Ted in the house. What would she do without it? She built a fire and stared into it. She seemed to be raising more questions than answers. Now personal questions added to the confusion. When had Ted gotten the vasectomy? Did he have affairs before Tina?

And Bill. Who the hell was he? Not even his friends knew what he did or even where he'd lived before moving to the beach. He'd arrived shortly after Tina. Was there a connection? *Oh damn,* she thought. *I've read way too many mystery and spy stories.*

But maybe she could learn from them. What would Sue Grafton's Kinsey Millhone do? Forget about Nancy Drew--she was dealing with adult problems. It'd be a lot easier to find the secret in the hidden staircase than to discover the answers to all of her questions.

How badly did she want the answers? Only enough to recover her new life at the beach and get rid of Ted. It was hard to believe that a week ago she had been sitting up here drinking a Cognac in total contentment, looking forward to her reinvented existence.

"Julie," Ted called. "Can you come down? Or I'll come up if you prefer. We need to talk."

"No, Ted. Don't come up. I'm on my way down," she said, rising up from the sofa and looking longingly at her sleeping Sheba.

"I'll trade you lives," she said as the cat opened one eye and looked at her quizzically.

She quickly descended both flights of stairs and stood at the bottom of the staircase looking at Ted.

"Thanks, Julie. Why don't you sit down. I think I need to explain about the vasectomy."

"Ted, it's been years. Does it really matter now that we're almost divorced?" Julie asked, remaining where she was.

"It does to me because I've been unfair to you, and I'd like a chance to get back in your good graces."

"My good graces. What does that mean?"

"It means I'm sorry. I didn't treat you very well. And, well, I've missed you."

"Let's not go there," she answered, moving toward the sofa and sitting across from him. "Tell me about the vasectomy, if you wish. I admit I'm curious."

"I got it over fifteen years ago," he said. "I knew your biological clock was ticking, and I didn't want to take any chances. I really couldn't face bringing a child into the world. I'd had such a rotten childhood. Living in one horrible foster home after another. Never getting adopted. Childhood was hell. Yours was great, and I knew you wouldn't understand. Besides, I had my career. It demanded a lot of time."

"Yes, it did. I never would've tricked you into fatherhood. I thought you knew me better than that. My childhood was pretty good, even though my parents divorced. I knew they both loved me. So, no, I didn't totally understand what your life was like. Tell me, though. Were there other affairs before Tina?"

Ted looked shocked. "Of course not. I never planned that. You've got to believe me. You were so busy with your work, and Tina was there every day. She was a fabulous assistant, and then when we got to know one another and I found out she'd gone from foster home to foster home, too, it seemed like we had a real understanding of one another. I didn't plan to fall in love with her. It just happened. I'm sorry. Now she's dead, and maybe we can . . . ."

"Stop it! Do you really believe I want you back after all that has happened? You're staying in my god-awful cottage, or whatever you referred to it as. I think our divorce was long overdue. I appreciate the explanation about the vasectomy, even though it came fifteen years too late." She stood up. " Now, if you'll excuse me, I think I'll go upstairs."

"Good night, Julie. Sleep on it. Maybe we can still make it work."

"Good night," she said, climbing back up the stairs. "Forget about us, please."

* * * * * * * * *

After coffee and toast in the morning, Julie bundled up for a walk on the beach. It was sunny but windy and a little chilly. Great weather for walking and clearing her head. She hoped that Bill would have some information for them from the fingerprint records, and the DNA results should be in. What would Ted do if he found out his vasectomy hadn't worked and he was the father?

She walked along the surf line, and as it was low tide, lots of beach debris was strewn in the wet sand. She found several pieces of beach glass and a really large sand dollar. She put the glass in her pocket and carefully held the sand dollar in her left hand where it wouldn't get broken. Robbie, Jenn's husband, was walking their lab again. She paused and said hello and patted the dog's head, before continuing her trek. Not too many people were out in this wind. She turned and headed back to her house.

She heard Ted on the phone as she entered. She hung up her jacket in the entry closet, stepped into the half bath, running her fingers through her hair as she looked in the mirror. Then she picked up her beach treasures and took them up to the window sills in the crow's nest.

"Julie," Ted said as she came back down. "That was the police department. The baby wasn't mine. I certainly didn't want a baby, but I wouldn't want my baby murdered, although somebody's baby is dead. Oh, I don't know what I mean. Anyway, that should take me off the hook for murder, don't you think?"

"How do you see that? Don't you think the police will think you were jealous that Tina'd been with another man and gotten pregnant, especially since you'd had a vasectomy and were pretty sure it wasn't yours? What about her ex? Has he had a DNA test?"

"Yes, but they wouldn't give me his results. I bet Don, or more likely Bill, can get them for us, don't you think?"

"Yeah, probably Bill. How do you think he does it? Gets all his information, I mean?" Julie asked.

"Well, he's a private eye. Can't they get things no one else can?"

"I'm not sure. Just curious." His methods did seem a little unusual, she thought. How did he get his information?

Since there was nothing else on their agenda until they heard from Bill, Julie decided to change and go into the real estate office for a while. She'd neglected her job for too long.

After half a day of returning phone calls, checking with escrow offices, and chatting with several of her colleagues, Julie returned home. Bill's truck was in the driveway, so she parked on the street.

"Hi, I'm home," she called as she opened the door. Bill and Ted were seated across from one another in the living room as she came in. She took another chair and joined them.

"What's the news?" she asked as she settled into the chair.

"Well," Ted said. "Bill's found out a little about Tina. She wasn't who we thought she was."

"Yeah," Bill added. "The fingerprinting got some interesting results making me wonder if she was involved in a government scheme for a new identity, you know, Witness Protection or something. Her real name was Theresa Fairchild, not Tina Randall. She's from New Jersey, not New York City. Usually, if the government's involved in creating a new identity, you can't find original driver's license information. But someone must have screwed up. Her prints were available showing she'd lived in a small town in New Jersey, a suburb outside of Atlantic City."

"Once I found her name, I located the high school where she graduated and even found college records for her in New Jersey again, not New York. She didn't graduate from college, however. She left her junior year. Just quit going. That's when Theresa effectively disappeared, and Tina showed up out west. There's a lot of crime in New Jersey. Made me wonder if she was an eye witness in an investigation and was given a new identity as protection. If that's the case, it didn't work too well, did it?"

"So that can help me, right?" Ted asked. "I'm innocent, and now I can prove it, can't I?"

"Wait a minute," Bill cautioned. "We have nothing to prove my conjectures are right. For all we know, she was involved in crime and came here with the mob providing an identity, or even more far-fetched, she's a spy of some sorts. We have no proof of anything, and the police department isn't going to buy it. No, we're going to have to do a ton more sleuthing before we have a case."

"But, you can do it, can't you, Bill?" Ted pleaded.

Bill looked from Ted to Julie. "I hope so," he said. "I hope so."

I hope so, too, she thought. *And soon.*

Chapter Eleven

Ted might be a genius at design, however, he wasn't much help in figuring things out. He had such simplistic thoughts, Julie mused. He really believed that they now had information that would get him off the hook, just as he'd thought that his not being the father of Tina's baby would take away doubt. No, he wasn't going to be of much assistance solving this problem. She was glad they had Bill working for them. Bill seemed to be able to get incredible information. He said he'd find out about Reggie's DNA test. Those results could make him the prime suspect.

She wondered what Tina had really been up to. Why had she married Reggie if she was on the run? Although maybe that was to give her an even better cover. Maybe Reggie was involved in the secret. Why did she come work for Ted? It was all so confusing. And why did she get killed in that brief half hour or so that Ted was out of the condo?

Looking at her calendar, Julie saw that yoga was going to start in an hour. That might be just what she needed to clear her head of this mess. She called Eleanor and told her she'd like to go.

Forty-five minutes later, Julie picked up Eleanor and Jenn and took off for the yoga studio, which was located upstairs over an art gallery on the river. As she walked in, she knew that just being in this room would help her relax her body and her mind. The views were soothing, the wood floors gleamed, myrtlewood incense burned, and soft music filled the air. The instructor was close to her age--a friendly, calm woman with long white hair pulled back in a braid down her back. Dressed all in white and barefoot, she looked the way a yogi should look--peaceful and spiritual.

Jenn introduced her saying, "Lana, this is Julie. She's new in town and eager to join our group."

"Welcome, Julie," Lana answered in a soft voice, bowing her head. "Namaste." She pointed to a space over by the window. "I think there's room over there. Jenn can help you get your mat in place. Be sure to grab a blanket."

They took their places on the mats on the floor. It was a good workout but not so strenuous that Julie felt fatigued. She loved listening to the gong Lana played so expertly during meditation--all thoughts and problems vanished. Tension had completely left her body. She was so relaxed her legs felt like spaghetti, and she wondered if it was safe for her to drive.

The walk down the stairs grounded her, so she was able to drive and feel like she was back in the real world. Until Eleanor asked her how things were going with Ted in the house, she'd completely forgotten about Ted, Tina, and murder.

"Well, it's not as bad as I thought it would be," she told Eleanor and Jenn. "Thank god I've got the crow's nest to escape to. It's entirely off limits to Ted. It's been wonderful to have my own sanctuary. Ted would like to get back together, but that's not going to happen," she added, sharing a little personal information but not willing to talk about the investigation or Bill's part in it.

She dropped them off and headed back down the street ready to deal with the world again. God, she hoped that the case would get solved soon. She really wanted her life back.

She was surprised that Bill was at her house when she came in. He and Ted were seated in the living room. Bill looked as appealing as ever in his close fitting jeans with the blue sweatshirt that made his eyes seem bluer than ever. He was one good-looking man. Poor Ted. He looked old and used up, with very little life in his face. He'd really aged in the past few days. Even his clothes, his real clothes that he'd rescued from the condo, drooped on him. He must have lost at least eight to ten pounds.

"Why hi, Bill," she said. "I didn't see your truck. You didn't make it to yoga today."

"No, I was waiting for the news from Reggie's test. And it was nice enough out I decided to jog down the beach. I really don't live that far away, and I needed the exercise," he said, patting his abs.

"He just got here and was about to tell me about Reggie's DNA results." Ted added, "Now you can hear, too."

Julie took a seat wondering whether it would matter much to their case.

"It turns out, he's not the father either," Bill said. "So there was obviously someone else in Tina's life. We found out that she was at the gym a lot--you know, Jake's Powerhouse. So maybe one of the guys there was involved with her."

"Have you found out who Bruno is?" Julie asked. "Although he really didn't look like her type. I imagine, however, he could be quite persuasive."

"Jeez," Ted said. " I can't believe Tina would sleep with him when she had me. What could she've been thinking?"

"We don't know who it was at this point," Bill reminded them. "And apparently this Bruno character wasn't around when my associate went to check out the gym. She's joined the gym, however, and expects to be a regular, so we'll see what she finds out."

"A female investigator," Julie said. "Good idea. How much staff do you have working for you?"

"Yes, I decided a woman asking questions wouldn't arouse as much attention as a man. My associates are mostly independent contractors. You know, hired on an as-needed basis. It's great to have a variety of contacts. Then they don't get known as my employees and find it hard to keep a cover."

"You sound pretty knowledgeable about all of this," Julie said, thinking it seemed like a pretty big operation. "How long have you been in the business?"

"Oh, it's a sideline I picked up after I was in the military," Bill answered. "I always liked to ask questions and find answers. It entertains me when I get the right case."

Boy, he still really never shares much, Julie thought, and then asked, "What branch of the service were you in?"

"Army, Special Forces," he answered. "Now, let's get back to what we're going to do next."

"I'm all ears," Julie said, and Ted nodded in agreement.

Bill told them he had a contact in New Jersey who was going to check out what was going on in the area when Theresa's identity changed to Tina. For example, any big murders, drug heists, etc., might help explain why she needed to become someone new.

"And," he added, "my associate at the gym is going to try to cultivate some friendships and see where that takes her. She's pretending to be a friend of Tina's and put Tina down as the person who recommended the gym to her when she registered. So far, no one has really said much about Tina. But she's going to gradually persist and also keep her eyes open for Bruno and others."

"That sounds like a good plan," Ted said. "I think the gym could somehow be involved."

"I still think you might be at risk," Bill told them. "Therefore, I've hired security to keep an eye on both of you and the house." Julie didn't bother to tell him that Jon and Phil could also easily keep an eye on the house, although, having been to their place, he was probably aware of that as well.

"Any ideas about what could be in the box that Bruno took?" Julie asked.

"Just guesses at this point," Bill responded. "Could be a DVD, CDs, papers, most anything. I don't think we'll know much until we can figure out why she changed her name and moved cross country. Oh, and here's her phone back in case the police department asks about it. You can say you found it in the office and forgot to give it to them. I doubt they'll believe you, but you should probably turn it in. I've erased any history that might show that it's been recently examined."

He set the phone on the coffee table, got up, and walked to the beachside door. "Hang tight," he said. "Security should start up in a couple of hours. If they do their job right, you won't even be aware of them. Bye." And he took off jogging over the dunes.

Again, Julie wondered why this was so important to Bill. He really was spending a great deal of time on Ted's case. Did he like her enough to be involved for her sake or was something else going on?

"Do you really think we need security, Jules?" Ted asked. "It seems pretty creepy to me."

"Dammit! The whole situation is pretty creepy, and I'd prefer not to have Bruno show up again, wouldn't you?"

She'd never realized he was such a crybaby, and now he was calling her Jules again, his nickname for her when they were married.

Julie marched up the stairs and settled on the sofa. She pulled out the book her mystery club was reading--the newest by Sue Grafton. Well, she hadn't caught up with Kinsey for awhile. This should take her away from the present.

Chapter Twelve

Julie was in the midst of Kinsey's investigation when the phone rang. It was Phil. He and Jon invited them to dinner. What a nice change, she thought. It would do them both good to get out of the house, and Ted would love their modern decor.

She went downstairs to ask Ted if he'd like to go. Ted looked up from the golf match on TV and agreed that it would be great to be around other people and not talk or think about the murder.

She raided the wine closet and found a nice Cabernet to take since Phil had said they were barbecuing steak. She wasn't a meat eater, but Ted was. She'd never had a problem filling up on salad and bread, and/or whatever side dish might be offered. No point telling them ahead of time that she was a vegetarian, or more accurately a pescatarian, since she did eat fish. Ted would enjoy steak for a change.

They walked across the street and up the front walk. Ted commented on the mid-century style and how it fit into the beach scene so well. She looked up. She could appreciate the glass and geometry, but it wasn't her.

Jon greeted them at the door and offered to show Ted around while she carried the wine upstairs to the kitchen. She quietly explained her veggie preference to Phil who said they tended to eat mostly fish and veggies themselves but splurged on an occasional steak. She assured him that Ted would be delighted. And she was looking forward to the evening as well.

They had a great time talking about surfing, living at the beach, modern decor, and the problems associated with teaching. The world of education was pretty foreign to both Julie and Ted, but they enjoyed the anecdotes and left with an appreciation of what a hard job those guys had.

As they walked home, Ted looked at her house and said, "You know. Your cottage is growing on me, Jules. I never thought I would like an old-fashioned house, but it's cozy and comfortable. Thanks again for taking me in."

"Well, thanks. Never thought I'd hear appreciation for an old, possibly drafty house from you. But I love it. It suits me, somehow."

As they opened the front door, they heard a crash upstairs.

Julie ran up the stairs as Ted yelled, "Julie. Stop! It could be dangerous. Where the hell is security?" And he ran back out the front door, calling for help.

Although her heart was racing, Julie paid no attention to him, but headed into Ted's bedroom, the room where the sound seemed to have come from. She turned on the overhead light and discovered the bedside lamp knocked over on the floor. As she was putting it back on the nightstand, Sheba came out from under the bed mewing.

So, it was only the cat. Julie picked her up and petted her as she came back down the stairs. Ted was still at the front door. He was talking to some man that Julie assumed was security even though he was dressed more like a beach bum than a guard. She guessed it was a good cover.

"It's okay," she told both of them. "It was only Sheba." She held the cat out for them to see. "She knocked over the lamp in Ted's room."

As they came back in, Ted chided her. "Why did you go up there? It could've been dangerous."

"I assumed that no one could get in if security was outside. In fact, I guess I really didn't think. I just wanted to find out what the noise was. It's okay. It really was just the cat."

"Let's have a cup of tea and sit down for a minute," Ted said. "I, for one, need to catch my breath."

"Okay. Me, too," Julie admitted. And she thought it really was rather nice to have someone worried about her, better than if she'd been alone. *However,* she told herself, *if I were alone and Ted weren't here, none of this awful stuff would be happening.* She went into the kitchen to plug in the electric kettle.

After sharing tea with Ted, Julie climbed to the crow's nest, retrieved her Grafton mystery, and carried the book to her bed. She was sleepy even after the excitement earlier in the evening. She'd had several glasses of wine at Phil and Jon's, and the sleepy time tea was beginning to have an effect on her.

So, after her getting-ready-for-bed routine, she'd slipped under the covers and opened the book. She'd only read a few pages when there was a knock on the door.

"Jules, are you awake?" Ted asked.

For Pete's sakes, what could he want?

"Yes," she responded. "What do you need?"

"Could I come in and talk to you?"

"I'm reading," she answered. "This isn't a good time."

The door opened slowly. Ted came over to the bed and sat down next to her. Before she realized what he was doing, he was embracing her.

"Jules, Jules," he moaned. "I'm so sorry. I still love you. I've made such a big mistake."

She had to admit it felt good to have his arms around her again, but she really didn't want Ted back in her life.

"Stop it!" she ordered firmly, pulling back. "This is not part of our deal. Get out. If you can't leave me alone, then you are going to have to move out immediately. Good night!" She pushed him off the bed. "Go back to your room, now."

"I'm sorry, Julie," he said standing up. "I miss you. Are you sure . . . ?"

"Ted," Julie answered, her voice demonstrating her mounting anger. "Leave. Right this minute."

He hastily walked to the door, turned to look at her one last time, then closed the door behind him.

Julie was wide awake now. What was happening to her? Part of her wanted him--the other part wanted him gone. She knew which part to listen to, but her heart was beating faster and not from fear this time. It'd been too long since a man had held her. And actually, it was Bill's arms she wanted around her.

She tried to get back into the story she was reading, but she couldn't concentrate. After she paced the room a few times, she decided a hot bath might relax her.

She moved into the bathroom, ran a hot tub, added lavender bubble bath, and climbed in to soak. As the warmth spread through her, she thought, *I've had so many changes in the past month. No wonder I'm confused.* She just wanted to get a good night's sleep and think about everything in the morning.

Julie's unconscious mind did not cooperate. She tossed restlessly all night, dreaming of erotic love-making, first with Ted and then with Bill. Suddenly Tina's bloody body was there, and then Bruno stood over her leering. She finally went to sleep with Kinsey whispering to her that she could do it, she could solve this crime. Easy for Kinsey to say.

Chapter Thirteen

The phone ringing by her bedside awoke her from whatever dreams had entered her late morning consciousness. She promptly lost them as she reached for the phone. It had stopped ringing, so she left it alone. Ted must have answered. She tried to cuddle back under the covers, but she was now wide awake, and Sheba was staring at her with that "feed me" look she had.

"Okay, okay," she told the cat. "See, I'm getting up."

She brushed her teeth, threw on jeans and a sweatshirt, and hurried down to the kitchen to feed the cat. Ted was still on the phone. Maybe it was someone from his office. But wouldn't they have used his cell?

After giving Sheba, her food, she poured some coffee and listened to Ted's end of the conversation.

"Wow! A mob killing? And you think she might've been a witness?"

Ted saw her and said into the phone, "Just a minute, Bill. Julie's up."

Then looking at her, he said, "Bill's found out about a big mob killing about the same time Theresa disappeared, moved west, and became Tina."

"Yeah, Bill. Yeah, I was just catching her up. Anything we can do?"

He listened for a minute, and then said, "Thanks. Here she is." He handed the phone to Julie.

"Hi, Bill," Julie said. "So there might be a mob connection?"

"Possibly," Bill replied. "We can't rule it out; however, we still need to make sure that there wasn't anything else going on that she could've been involved with. Now, here's the reason I asked to talk to you. Look outside. It's gorgeous. How about a paddle in about an hour? I think it would be good for both of us to get out on the water. What do you think?"

Kayaking sounded perfect, and she really did want to spend more time with Bill--alone, just the two of them.

Julie answered immediately. "You're so right. I'd love to, Bill. See you in an hour." As she looked up, she knew that Ted would be pissed, but too bad. She needed some time away from him.

"So, what would you love to do?" Ted asked, as Julie hung up the phone.

"I'm going kayaking," she answered.

"Hey, I'd like to try that," he said.

"Sorry. You weren't invited. And Bill's only got two kayaks as far as I know. I moved to the beach to have some fun, and I'm going to go enjoy myself. Find something to do while I'm gone. Okay?"

Ted stormed off out the glass door to the beach. She watched him stomping over the dunes. God, she needed a break.

When Bill arrived, she helped him stow the blue boat in the back of his pickup, and they set off.

As they paddled on another small lake, Julie leaned back in her kayak and breathed the sweet air. *Now this is what paradise is like*, she thought. She needed more days floating on the water.

"Thank you, Bill. You don't know what a god-send you were. I've been cooped up in that house far too long with Ted. I really needed to get out. This is absolutely wonderful." She looked over to his kayak into those Redford eyes feeling at that moment that she would go anywhere he wanted, do anything he suggested.

"I'm glad, Julie. But I also need to talk to you about the case before we go back. It can wait, but there are some things we need to discuss without Ted."

"Okay. But later, please?" *Please,* she thought to herself. She just wanted this time on the lake to be about them, the beautiful day, and being out on the water together.

"Sure," he said, and pointed out a beaver's dam on an small inlet.

When they finally started heading back to the dock, Julie said, "Okay. Let's talk."

"Julie, are you positive that Ted didn't do it? The evidence looks pretty damning. The police are going to be arresting him in the next few days if we can't come up with something. Are we delaying the inevitable?"

Julie paused. She'd wondered this herself but didn't really believe Ted was capable of murder.

"I don't think he had a motive," she began. "I really think he was shocked about the pregnancy. Whether he knew Tina had another guy, I don't know. But I don't think that would lead him to kill her. I think he'd probably throw her out and fire her as his assistant. But murder? And with a knife? I think if Ted were going to kill someone, it'd be with poison, or he'd hire someone. . . oh, he could've hired someone who knew he was going to be out. That's what you're hinting at, isn't it?"

"I still don't know. But you seem pretty rational. I really wanted to know what you think. Has the idea of an accomplice just now occurred to you?"

"Honestly, yes. That changes things, doesn't it? But does it explain Tina and her hidden identity? Aren't we better following that lead?"

"I don't intend to close any doors at present. Just wanted to share the possibilities," he said, as they paddled up the ramp.

Julie's peace had left her. They loaded the kayaks in the back of the truck and drove home. As she sat in the truck, she wondered if

Ted could possibly have hired someone to kill Tina. But wouldn't he have spoken to someone or done something to prove an alibi?

* * * * * * * * * *

Because both Julie and Ted needed to go to the city Monday, they got up early. Julie had to run by her old office and sign some forms. Ted wanted to go to his office and the condo. His car had finally been released, so they could pick that up as well.

They stopped at her office first. Ted stayed in the car while she signed the documents, and then they left for his business. She waited in the car in the parking garage as he went in to take care of a few things. She looked around cautiously and checked to make sure the doors were locked. She'd brought a book along to keep her company. She was just reaching for it when a movement caught her eye. Someone big, Bruno maybe, was coming out of the elevator next to the one Ted had just gone up in. She wondered what he was doing in this building if he'd gotten what he wanted from them before.

Without thinking about what she was doing, Julie quietly slipped out of the car, shutting the door softly. Bruno paid no attention to her and sauntered out the exit. So, he didn't have a car here. She followed him down the street and saw him go into Jake's Powerhouse, the gym that Bill had mentioned. She waited a few minutes and then went in herself.

The receptionist, a no-nonsense looking redhead with large tattooed arms said, "I'm Shirley. Can I help you?"

Julie responded, "Yes. I've been thinking about building up some muscles. I'd like to talk with you about joining."

As the receptionist explained the membership procedures and showed her some brochures, Julie positioned herself so that she could see through the glass doors into the main gym. No sign of the Bruno guy. The equipment looked daunting--a few ellipticals, bicycles, and treadmills, but lots of weight benches with racks of big heavy weights. No sissy aerobic or zumba classes here, she mused.

What the hell, she thought. *I could use some muscles.* She signed up for a month and asked for a tour. As they pushed through the glass doors, the smell of sweat was overpowering. Shirley pointed out several machines Julie could use. Sure, she thought, she could kill herself just getting on one of those.

As they neared the boxing ring, not in use at the moment, Shirley said, "Lots of women are taking up boxing. We give classes. Might be good for you."

Not a sport Julie was interested in. She shook her head, saying, " I don't think that's for me."

She would come back, however, not only to take advantage of the membership but to listen to others in the gym and see if she could learn anything about either Tina or Bruno. She knew Bill's associate would be doing the same thing, but she couldn't be here all the time. Maybe she'd learn something helpful.

As she left, she thanked Shirley and said she would be back later with her gym clothes, ready to work out. She walked down the street to the garage where Ted was standing by the car looking angry.

"Where the hell were you?" he asked. "You left the car locked, and I had to stand here waiting for you."

"Oh, I just went for a short walk," she answered. "Sorry."

The lot where Ted's blue Audi TT Roadster had been stored was their next stop. She was so happy that he'd have his own wheels again. Playing chauffeur was not on her agenda. She happily dropped him off. He was going to the condo next and would meet her at her house for dinner.

She drove to an athletic-wear store recommended by Shirley, bought some workout clothes and shoes, and went back to the gym. Since she had a permit to park in Ted's lot, she parked there again, near the exit. She strolled back to the gym wondering what she'd find out.

Julie checked in with Shirley, was given a lock for her locker, and went to the changing room. Once she was in her workout clothes, she entered the training area. The acrid smell of sweat was so strong, she wiped her nose, looking around. About ten guys, no women, were working hard lifting weights. They barely looked at her. Bruno was not among them.

Toby, the trainer to whom she'd been assigned, noted the nose move and said, "You'll get used to the smell. In fact, in time it'll smell like home."

I don't think so, she said to herself. *Not my home anyway.*

Toby was a small but very powerfully built young man with a shaved head who sported the apparently de riguer wife-beater tee shirt which showed off his tattoos. He looked like a smaller version of Bruno.

As he demonstrated the equipment, set the weights, and had her try out the machines, she knew she was going to be really sore in the morning. Her muscles hadn't had a workout like this in years, if ever.

She saw no sign of Bruno, nor did she see or hear anything unusual while she was working out. This may have been a royal waste of money, she thought.

Julie was the only woman in the dressing room when she went into the shower. However, when she came back, a young woman, with huge biceps and shoulders, was changing into gym attire.

"Hi," Julie said. "You look like you've been coming here a long time. Wow."

The woman looked at her curiously, as if she knew Julie didn't belong.

"Yeah," she said. "I've been body building for several years. Just won a contest. What brings you here?"

"I'm Julie," she said, extending her hand. "I work downtown and just want to build some muscle. I don't intend to get as serious as you, but I would like a better body." That wasn't a lie. She really would like a better body.

"I'm Darcy," was the reply as the woman firmly shook hands with Julie. Julie noticed several tattoos on her forearms and neck.

She wondered if getting a tattoo was a requirement for working out here.

"If you stay with it, you'll see improvements pretty soon. And you never know, you may decide to enter competitions in your age group in a year's time."

"I don't know about the competitions, but I do hope to see improvements before long," Julie replied. Then she asked, "Do you know some of the other women who are regulars? I'm looking for the woman who told me about this place. Can't remember her name. She's small, young, like you, long blonde hair, great shape, no visible tattoos."

"Oh, that sounds like Tina. You must not've seen the news. She was killed by her boyfriend. It's been on the TV. Killed with a knife. Sounded awful. She used to come in a lot. May have dated a couple of the guys here. Could be that's why her boyfriend did away with her."

"Oh, how terrible. I didn't really know her. Just saw her on the elevator a few times. Who were the guys she might've dated?"

Darcy looked at her curiously. "Marcus and Vic," she said. "Why do you ask?"

"Oh I saw her on the elevator with a guy once who looked like he worked out. Big, huge, bald guy with a tattoo on his right arm--dragon or maybe a snake. Know him?"

"That sounds like Vic. I'd stay away from him if I was you. He's got a bad temper. Well, I need to hit the equipment. Good luck with your muscles tomorrow. I suggest a hot bath tonight to relax them."

"Thanks. I'll remember that. Nice meeting you," Julie said as she finished dressing. After applying her make-up and brushing her hair, she headed out the door.

So, it sounded like Bruno was really named Vic. And Tina had possibly dated him. Did this really help or not? She clicked her car unlocked as she neared it. Suddenly she felt big hands over her mouth as the hulk, probably Vic, forced her toward the car.

She struggled, but he was way too much for her. He grabbed her keys out of her hand, cuffed her hands behind her with some kind of wire, threw her into the passenger seat, and strapped the seat belt across her.

"Don't move, bitch," he said as he walked around to the driver's seat.

Chapter Fourteen

Don't move. He had to be kidding. As if she were capable of doing anything with her hands behind her and strapped into the seat. She could scream, but no one else was in the parking garage. Ted wouldn't even know she was missing until she didn't show up at home for dinner.

"Please, Mr. uh, uh . . . Don't hurt me. I haven't done anything to you."

"Shuddup," he answered. "I don't need people lookin' for me at the gym or anywhere else. You don't look the type for Jake's Powerhouse. What're you doin' there? And don't lie to me."

"Well, it was close to Ted's work," she said meekly. "And I thought I could get some exercise when I was in town. I did work out with a trainer today."

"But you asked Darcy 'bout me. How come?" he demanded.

Shit. That was stupid, Julie thought. Darcy'd told him she was asking about him.

She noticed they were heading into the mountains toward the beach. Perhaps he'd take her home when he was through questioning her. More likely. though, he'd kill her and leave her body in the forest for the bears or mountain lions. She shivered.

"Lady, I asked you a question. Why're you askin' 'bout me?"

"Well, I'm sure that you know that Tina was living with Ted. I'm trying to help get him off the hook and was just trying to find out who else she might have been involved with. Darcy thought you might have dated her."

"Dated. That's a laugh. We didn't date; we fucked. Does that answer your question?"

"So you could've been the father?" Julie asked.

"What father? What the hell you talkin' 'bout?"

"Uh, you didn't know she was pregnant?" Julie asked.

"Tina? Preggars? Nah, Tina knew how to take care of herself. She couldn't of been pregnant."

"Well, she was," Julie answered. "The cops did a DNA test, and it wasn't Ted's baby or her ex-husband's. So maybe that leaves you."

"What'm I goin' to do with you?" Vic asked. "You sure got a big mouth on you and maybe know a little too much."

"Me? You can take me home," Julie said as calmly as she could. "I don't know anything else, and I don't want to know anything. Please take me home. I promise I won't say a word about you to anyone."

"Yeah. That's what I told you to do before. And look what happened? You butted into my business. No, I think I'm goin' to haff to dispose of you."

"Dis. . . pose of me?" Julie questioned. "But couldn't you get in trouble for that? You don't need murder on your hands."

"Listen lady, you've no idea how dirty my hands are already. So don't try and threaten me."

Adrenaline had kept her going for a while. But now she knew she was going to die. Terror mixed with sweat, and she was shaking uncontrollably. No one even knew she was out here. God, what would he do to her before he killed her? He looked like a monster and probably was.

Vic began slowing down as if looking for a turnoff. He pulled onto a logging road on the right. As the car bumped along the dirt road, Julie tried to think of a plan.

"I could pay you," she offered. "I bet you do things for money, don't you? How much would it be worth to you not to kill me?"

"Lady, you don't have that kind of money," he said. "I'm gettin' paid more than you can imagine to take you out."

He's being paid to take me out, she thought. Someone else is behind this. Who?

"So who wants me gone?" she asked. Not that it would matter. She probably wouldn't live long enough to tell anyone.

"None of your business," he said, pulling the car to a turnout at the edge of a cliff. *Jeez, he's going to leave me in the car and push it over the embankment.*

As Vic got out and walked behind the car around to the passenger door, she caught a glimpse of someone in the side view mirror. Was it a hiker? A hunter? She didn't care. She began to scream at the top of her lungs and managed to get her foot on the horn. Too bad her hands weren't free. But the beeping horn had startled Vic, who turned around just in time to receive a blow to his skull from a weapon, maybe a gun. It was hard to see in the mirror.

Now Vic was down, and the stranger approached her car door. He was a tall, thin, young man who was dressed in hiking boots and shorts with a small backpack. Her first thought was that he was a Boy Scout. Anyway, he'd certainly come to her rescue.

"Problem with your boyfriend, Ma'am?" he asked.

"Boyfriend? Oh that's no boyfriend of mine. He was going to murder me. I can't tell you how fortunate I feel. Can you uncuff my hands please? You'll have to undo the seat belt first."

As the stranger bent over her to help her, she glanced in the mirror again and saw Vic slink away into the woods.

"He's getting away," she said. "What are we going to do?"

"Well, little lady, I've got his gun. We're going to put you in the driver's seat and have you drive right out of here. I'll take care of him. Now get home, Julie," he muttered.

Julie? He knows my name.

"Who are you?" she demanded.

"Doesn't matter. Just get over to the driver's seat and get the hell out of here."

As curious as she was, Julie sensibly complied and was soon bouncing back toward the highway. She was still shaking, but she sure didn't want to stop out here. She didn't see the stranger's car and wondered where he'd parked and how he'd known her name.

It was late afternoon when she returned home. Ted wasn't even back yet. She decided to call Bill and find out if he knew anything. Again she was puzzled. How had that stranger known who she was?

"Bill. It's Julie," she said when he answered.

"About time you were back," he said. "I'll be right over."

After she hung up, she went into the kitchen and made herself a pot of tea. Her hands weren't visibly shaking, but she was still quaking on the inside.

Bill showed up at the front door on the street side, so he must have driven.

"Hi, Bill. I'm having tea. Want some, or a drink?" she asked.

"No, thanks, Julie," he responded. "What the hell were you doing nosing around the gym? Didn't I tell you I had it staked out? Vic could have killed you if I hadn't had you tailed."

"Vic did almost kill me until I was rescued by a hiker. Oh," she said, realizing how the man knew her name. "That was the tail who rescued me, wasn't he? What did he do to Vic?"

"None of your business," Bill said. "Just keep your nose out of this. We're still trying to figure out who the players are and what this is about. I don't need to be rescuing you at the same time."

"Sorry," she answered. "I really am. And thanks for keeping an eye on me. Is there anything you can tell me?"

"Just that this appears to be a lot bigger than we thought. It looks like Ted is just a scapegoat, and if he becomes a liability, they'll get rid of him. So, it behooves him to remain the chief suspect for a while longer. Get it?"

"Yeah," she said. "Sorry again."

"I don't really blame you for wanting to help him. But just stay out of it," he said. "Now I'm going to head home. Bye."

"Bye," she replied. "Thanks."

Well, he was certainly pissed at her. Again she wondered why this was so important to him. He hadn't seemed sympathetic to her, just angry that she'd gotten involved.

Dammit. Ted was her problem, not Bill's. Okay, Ted had hired him. But she had a right to get involved if she wanted to. She also had to admit that he was correct--she was definitely in over her head. If only she could truly believe his motives.

Julie took her cup of tea with her upstairs and settled into her tub for a long, hot soak.

Chapter Fifteen

By the time Ted came in, she was dressed in her comfortable sweats and sipping her scotch, stretched out on the living room. sofa.

"Hi," he announced. "I just parked my TT in the driveway for now. I can move it if you need to get your car out. My day was fine. I got a lot accomplished. How about you?"

"Oh," Julie said, sitting up. "I forgot about parking your car. It should be okay in the driveway tonight. We can rearrange things tomorrow if we need to. Why don't you pour yourself a drink before I tell you what happened to me."

Ted raised his eyebrows as if to question her but quickly went into the kitchen and made a scotch and water.

"So," he asked, moving across from her to sit on one of the chairs. "What happened?"

As she related the story of going to the gym, being kidnapped, and finding herself alone with Vic on an old logging road in the mountains, she could see Ted stare at her as if he couldn't really believe what had happened. He finally let out his breath as she explained her rescue.

"Boy, you were lucky that hiker came along," he said. "I couldn't bear if anything happened to you. Please don't do anything that will put you in danger. This is all my fault. I'm so sorry."

"Well, it isn't really all your fault, except for getting involved with Tina. That is your fault. But you didn't know she was mixed up in crime. Oh, and the hiker wasn't real. He was the tail that Bill put on me. Bill was pretty angry that I had gone to the gym asking about Vic. I wonder what that guy did to Vic? God, I hope he found him again. Vic was getting away on foot. Not sure where the tail had parked his car. But he must've caught up with Vic again because Bill knew all about it by the time I got home. You don't think he murdered Vic, do you?"

"Sounds like Vic should be killed by someone. He's one dangerous character. And Tina was really sleeping with him?"

"Maybe," Julie answered. "That's what he said anyhow. But he likes to brag, I think. If he was sleeping with her, it sounded more like intimidation than love. He probably threatened her. I just wonder how she was involved."

"Me, too. I still can't believe she had this whole other life and identity. Where did I fit in? Did she even love me? I should never have left you, Jules."

But if he hadn't, she thought, then she wouldn't have moved and started this new life.

"No, you shouldn't have left--not the way you did--for someone else. But let's face it. We were over. Our marriage hadn't been a real marriage for a long time. Neither of us was happy. We should have split up long ago, but neither of us had the courage to do it. Anyway, worrying about who did what isn't going to help us now. What're we going to do?"

"I don't know," Ted said. "But for now, why don't I fix dinner? You can just sit here and try to relax. You've had a really tough day and deserve a little pampering. Do you need a refill?"

"Thanks," she answered handing him her glass. "That would be great."

Ted walked out to the kitchen. When he returned, he handed her the drink and said, "Hey, we've got the crab I picked up yesterday. How about I make some of my famous crab chowder? That's good comfort food."

"That sounds absolutely wonderful," she answered.

As she stretched out on the sofa, she wondered what Bill wasn't telling her. Why was he involved? He had to be getting something out of this more than a paycheck. Was it because he was beginning to care about her? Was he with the government? Could he be working for the mob trying to find something that Ted didn't know he had or knew? Could Vic have been working for him and the rescue been a set-up to keep her guessing? More importantly, who the hell was Tina? What was her reason for changing her identity and moving west? And why Ted? Why did she latch on to him?

She and Ted didn't have much conversation over dinner. Julie said she needed an early night to herself. When she got to her room, she put on her pajamas and climbed up the stairs to her nest. She realized that she still hadn't checked on Bill.

After she turned on her laptop, she googled his name. A little information surfaced about him--mostly surfing tournaments he'd won. She put in the name of his detective agency. Nothing. Then she signed up on one of those investigative sites where you pay $29.95 to get information on people. She found out he was fifty-two years old and had served for twenty-five years in the Army, Special Forces.

This was interesting. He was born and raised in the same suburb of Atlantic City as Tina, only of course, he was more than a generation older. His dad was a cop; he had one older brother. She wondered if he'd known Tina's family. She found Bill's current address, phone number, etc. Nothing that she didn't already know except the possible New Jersey connection. What could that mean?

Why was it that the more involved she got in this case, the more questions she had? For every one possible answer, it seemed that at least three more questions arose. How did people do this for a living without going crazy? Bill was right. She should leave sleuthing to the professionals. Of course, that was only if she could trust Bill.

Now that she was on-line, she decided to invest another $29.95 and see what turned up about Thersa Fairchild, Tina's real name. Well, well, well. She hadn't been an orphan at all, and she'd grown up on the same street as Bill. Again, did that mean anything? She wasn't even born when he lived there. But maybe his parents had still lived there and knew her family. This was just a little too cozy. Too many Jersey connections all the way around.

Bill was truthful when he said that information about Theresa ended when she was twenty. She'd gone to college locally and then disappeared. No new data on her at all.

She tried to remember what she knew about Witness Protection Programs. Mostly what she'd seen on TV. Usually it involved an eye witness in a federal case. The government promised a new identity in exchange for testimony.

This internet research was getting fun. She went back to the year that Theresa had disappeared, found the Atlantic City newspaper, and searched for "gangsters." Sure enough. There was a headline about a trial for a mob boss named Sonny Turso. Wow, he'd probably killed at least a dozen people: he was involved in drugs, money laundering, Ponzi schemes, and other criminal activities. But he was being charged with one murder. An eyewitness had been located who saw him shoot a man in cold-blood. Not only that, papers that tied him to the Ponzi scheme were missing along with some possible evidence in a sex ring. It was conjectured that the witness had them. Apparently, she'd worked part time for an art gallery that appeared to be a front for the mob. The gallery accountant had been murdered in his office, which was then ransacked by the killer.

She scanned the articles. Sonny was supposed to go to trial, but the eyewitness, a college girl who'd been in the gallery at the time, had disappeared. No one could find her. Eventually Sonny Turso was released. No solid evidence to hold him.

This sounded like either the mob had helped her get away so she wouldn't testify, or, more likely, she'd disappeared on her own before they could kill her. Maybe she'd taken the records with her for protection.

Jeez, she and Ted were playing around with genuine gangsters. This wasn't a TV drama. This was real.

So what was Bill's connection? She jotted down some notes.

(1) He could be who and what he says he is

(2) He could be employed by the mob to get to Tina and get the evidence back

(3) He could be working for the government to find the evidence to put Sonny away

(4) Who knows?

So, if Bill wasn't who and what he said he was, they were in danger. If they worked with Bill, they could find themselves being used by the mob or by the government. Either way seemed dangerous. Although, if it had to be one or the other, she hoped he worked for the government. She was beginning to like Bill--a lot.

Chapter Sixteen

Another question that wouldn't go away was what was in the box Vic had taken from Tina's office? If that box contained the missing records, what were they looking for now? Was it possible that the box contained only a copy of the records, and they still needed to know where the originals were? Did Tina possess some other proof that Sonny killed the accountant?

The only thing that Julie totally understood was that she and Ted could not trust Bill one hundred percent. If he were working for the mob and leading them on, they were not safe at all. So what could they do to protect themselves? Their security was hired by Bill, maybe the mob, and answered to him. Suddenly she didn't feel so safe. There was no one to protect her. Ted was useless. In fact, he would never even think about these possibilities. No point telling him and frightening him further.

She wondered what it would take to get a gun. She used to be a pretty good shot. She'd never hunted with her dad, but she'd loved going to the shooting range with him and was pretty accurate. It probably wouldn't take her long to get back into it.

Yes, that was one positive thing she could do. Go apply for a gun permit and get a gun as soon as possible. What could she do in the meantime? Get a dog? But she didn't want a dog. She'd never wanted to be tied down to one. Cats were more her style. Unfortunately, Sheba wasn't much protection. She'd think about the dog. Also, she'd never had the locks changed after she purchased her home. She'd get an alarm system installed and new locks. She knew that wouldn't stop those thugs if they were really after her. But it might slow them down, give her time to get a gun out.

As she pushed away from the computer, she stood at the window that faced the street and saw Phil and Jon's home. They would help. She'd take them into her confidence. No, she wouldn't tell them about Bill and his interest in the case, but she'd tell them enough about Tina to indicate possible mob involvement and ask them to help keep an eye on her house. They had a bird's eye view of the front. It certainly wouldn't hurt to alert them. They could always call the sheriff's office if they saw anything suspicious. However, she knew it could take hours for the deputies to show up as they had hundreds of miles to patrol--the major problem with living rurally. That was scary.

She felt like she was putting tiny band-aids on a gushing artery. How much difference would any of this make if the mob decided to take them out? None. But somehow just brainstorming possibilities made her feel more powerful. And who knows, she might come up with a really good idea if she slept on it. If she could sleep.

Actually, she did sleep well. It might have been the ibuprofen she took to help her muscles that were beginning to ache. Or it might have been the loss of all the adrenaline she'd used during her encounter with Vic. But she awoke to a sunny morning feeling pretty invincible.

Ted had apparently slept well, too. Over breakfast she told him her thoughts about getting an alarm system and locksmith, but didn't share what she'd learned on the internet. She also didn't want him to know that she wasn't sure if they could have full faith in Bill. She was afraid he might let Bill know that she no longer trusted him, or Ted might act strangely around him. She needed Bill to believe that her confidence was still there--that she trusted him implicitly. And, if he really was working for them, that's what he needed to know. She just planned to be a lot more alert.

She read the paper thoroughly when Ted was through. Nothing about someone named Vic or anyone matching his description being found dead in a canyon. Of course, they could have disposed of the body in such a way it would never be found.

Maybe she would stake out the gym, not go in, but see if he was still around. Julie wasn't sure why that was important to know. But it seemed to be.

She told Ted she was going into the city to her office to clear up some loose ends. Unfortunately, he suggested that they take one car in, and he'd go do some work at his office. Actually, she decided maybe that wasn't such a bad idea. They could take his car, which maybe Vic wouldn't recognize. He'd sure know her car. Anyway, she'd park it down the street and sit in the coffee shop across the street from the gym. She'd take her book, sit by the window, read, drink coffee, and see who entered and exited the gym. And she'd call a locksmith and an alarm company.

She convinced Ted that his car was a better choice, reminding him that Vic had been in hers, and dropped him off at his office. She told him she was going to work, but promptly drove around the corner, managed to find a parking place close to the coffee shop, and went in. There were tons of tables available at 10:30 in the morning, so she bought coffee and a bagel and settled down in front of the window. She opened her book, stared out over it at the gym, remembering to turn the pages every so often, as she ate her bagel and sipped her coffee.

She noticed quite a number of people entering and leaving the gym during the next hour. One guy, from the rear, looked a lot like Vic, but when he turned sideways, his profile was wrong. She wondered if that was Reggie, Tina's ex-husband. Really a lot of big bruisers and a few women she wouldn't want to tangle with were clients there.

The lunch crowd was starting to build up. She just realized that she'd need to give up the table or order food when Ted came through the door.

"Julie," he asked, "what are you doing here? I thought I'd take a break and get some lunch."

"Me, too," she said. "Didn't know you came here to eat."

"Not often, but it's handy. Did you get your work done?"

"Yes, I did," she lied. "I only had to sign one set of documents, so I drove here. I've been reading my book."

"Well, let's order," Ted said. "I'd recommend the BLT, but you don't eat bacon."

"Actually, I think I'll have the avocado and cheese sandwich," she replied. "How about you? Are you caught up?"

"Not really. I've totally let work slide, and I have lots to do. Do you have things to keep you busy for another couple of hours?"

"Sure," Julie replied. "I may do a little window shopping." *And gun shopping,* she thought to herself.

They enjoyed a typical diner lunch, filling, comforting, but no presentation or style. Then Ted paid the bill and headed back up the street to his office. Julie had glanced out the window from time to time but still hadn't spotted Vic. Oh, well, she thought. He didn't necessarily live at the gym. She collected her belongings, got in the TT, and noticed a gun shop about a block away. Perfect, she thought.

Her computer research had indicated that no permit was needed in Oregon if she intended to keep the weapon in her home. And the purchase could be made immediately.

She drove down to the next block, parked, and walked to the gun shop, which was actually a really big hunting and sporting goods store. She found the gun counter at the back and located a small revolver which felt good in her hands. It was scary how simple it was to buy a gun. The whole process took about fifteen minutes. The dealer completed a form indicating what she'd bought and when, she signed it, answered no to a bunch of questions about previous criminal behaviors, gave her thumbprint, and provided her address. He then phoned the Department of the State Police who verified she had no criminal history.

She got some ammo, paid for everything, and the gun was hers. It was amazing how quickly someone could purchase a gun.

The salesman reminded her she needed a permit if she intended to carry it concealed on her person or vehicle. She told him that it was for home protection, but she did ask about taking it to a gun range. He said that as long as it was in a bag and in the back of her car, she could transport it back and forth.

He provided Julie with a list of gun ranges. One was located on the coast not far from her home where she could take a lesson and have some shooting practice. She wasn't sure how she felt about the ease of the whole process. But, she now had her weapon.

When she got back to the car, she put the package in the small trunk, drove to Ted's office, and parked in the garage. She moved to the passenger seat, locked the car door, and called Ted to let him know she was there. She told him not to hurry. She had her book and a few phone calls to make.

Julie spent the next twenty minutes arranging appointments with a locksmith and a security company for the next afternoon. She then called the gun club and got information about fees and times to take lessons. She scheduled a lesson for the next morning and was told she should bring her own gun with her to practice so she could learn how to use it.

She'd just finished her last call when Ted knocked on the window. She unlocked the door and let him in.

He was in pretty good spirits as he hummed along with the one radio station he could get. He seemed to enjoy being behind the wheel of his sports car and said he'd had a productive time but needed to go back the next day.

"That's fine, Ted." Julie said. "You can drive in on your own. I've got a ton of things to do at home."

When they pulled into the driveway, she asked him to open the trunk, got her purchase, unlocked the house door, and headed up the stairs. She stashed the parcel with the gun and ammo in her closet, freshened up, and joined Ted downstairs.

They chatted through dinner, watched a little TV together, and then she went upstairs.

Ted's good mood lasted until bedtime when he came to her room to say good night. She put down her book, firmly replied "Good night," knowing full well why he'd come to her room, and stared back at the book in front of her. Ted finally got the hint, sighed, and closed the door.

Chapter Seventeen

When she came down in the morning with Sheba meowing at her heels, Ted had already left for the city. Good. His note said not to expect him back until dinner. Great. She had the whole day to get everything done with no questions or interruptions.

After breakfast, she walked over to Phil and Jon's. Phil was out, but Jon invited her in. She stood in their living room looking down at her house.

"Jon," she began. "I want to ask a favor."

"Sure," he replied.

"Well, I know that you can easily see my driveway and front door," she began.

"Oh, believe, me," he interrupted. "We try to avoid looking at your house. What goes on there is none of our business."

"That's not what I meant," she said. "We may have some uninvited guests due to this murder case. I'm having new locks put on later today, and I'm installing a security system. I would really appreciate it if you would keep an eye on the house and call me or the sheriff if you notice anyone who shouldn't be there, or anything that's at all strange. Would you mind?"

"Gosh, we don't live by the windows, but we'll be happy to help out when we can," he said, rubbing his goatee. "Are you okay?"

"We're fine," she answered. "Just extra precautions. And please don't tell anybody except Phil. I don't want to worry our neighbors."

"Sure. No problem. I did see someone the other night after you left, but then Ted came out and was talking to him."

Oh, she thought. That's when Ted called out for security after Sheba knocked over the lamp. "Uh, I think that was when a client of Ted's stopped by to drop something off. He couldn't stay."

Jon looked at her as if he didn't quite believe her. Julie knew they both realized there had been no car, but he nodded.

"You do remember that we're going to Europe in a month. But until then, we'll be glad to help in any way we can. Hopefully, the case will be solved by then."

They chatted for a few minutes more, then Julie went home, put her gun and ammo in a duffel bag which she then placed in the back of her car, and headed for the gun range.

After she registered and paid, she met her instructor, a young woman named April. She looked about sixteen with her long, dark hair hanging down in two braids. Actually, she said she was twenty-five. She was a very competent teacher who spent quite a while showing Julie how to break down her weapon, clean it, and load it. April had her practice several times. She was starting to remember how to do this. Then they entered the shooting range itself.

They both were handed ear muffs to put on to help block the noise. April reminded her again what to do. She then covered her ears. She fired. She was within the target area. Good. It was coming back.

She opted for bull's eye targets. She practiced for about twenty minutes, actually hitting the center of the target several times. Then she unloaded her revolver and put it back in the bag with the ammo. As she drove home, she knew she would sleep better at night knowing the gun was in her bedside table.

* * * * * * * * *

She fixed a light lunch and took it out to the front garden where she was sheltered from the wind. She sat in the periwinkle adirondack chair the owners had left and collapsed in the warmth of the sun. She dozed for about twenty minutes and was awakened when the locksmith pulled into the driveway.

Picking up her plate and glass, she went to meet him. He followed her to the front door while she took her dishes to the kitchen. He examined the current locks and explained why a deadbolt would be far superior. Next he inspected the patio door to the ocean and told her about a keypad lock that would work there so she wouldn't need to take a key when she went out to the beach. He then showed her clips she could use on the windows. She agreed to all of his suggestions and left him to his work while she puttered in the kitchen. An hour later he was done. She had new locks, new keys, and a better level of protection than before.

However, when the security company arrived to discuss her options, she really felt she would be ratcheting up her safety. After she explained that she'd had an intruder and that she wanted the best system he could put in, they went from room to room. He shared numerous options, especially ones that her cat couldn't set off. By the time he left, she'd signed a contract for both the installation and a monthly service fee to monitor the system. He said he could install the system in two days, if that would fit her schedule. Julie agreed. It felt good to be making decisions.

She had forgotten to warn Ted about the new locks. She heard him try his key several times before she got to the door.

"I'm sorry," she told him. "I had the locks changed today. Oh, and we're getting a security system installed in a couple of days. I meant to do this when I first moved in but procrastinated. I think we'll both feel safer, don't you?"

He nodded in agreement. She then went to the kitchen and fetched a key for him which he promptly put on his keychain.

"I'm sure it's a good idea with you living out here alone," he said. "I'm glad you're doing it. By the way, have you heard any more from Bill? Don't you think we should have some news from him soon?"

"You know, I was wondering the same thing," Julie answered. "Why don't you give him a call?"

"Sure, in a couple of minutes. Hey, let's make reservations at that cute fish house on the river? Okay?"

"Sounds good to me," Julie said. "I certainly don't feel like cooking tonight. I'm going upstairs for now. See you in a while."

She poured herself some lemonade and climbed the stairs to the crow's nest, stopping by her bedside table to pick up her book. Book club met in a couple of days, and she was only halfway through. What was taking her so long?

As she picked it up and started reading, it suddenly dawned on her--Kinsey didn't age, well at least not the way normal people do in real time. When she'd read the first in the series, *A IS FOR ALIBI,* in the early eighties, she and Kinsey were about the same age--their early to mid-thirties. She flipped back to the front of *W Is for Witness* and skimmed a few pages. There it was. Kinsey was only in her late thirties. She'd aged maybe five or six years. In that same twenty years or so, Julie'd actually aged twenty years, was now fifty-five, and of course, didn't have the same outlook anymore.

Jeez, I'd thought Nancy Drew was too young for me to compare myself to, but so is Kinsey Millhone. She looked at the book again. Maybe now she could finish it, realizing Kinsey was just a young woman--not like Julie at all. So who could be a good detecting role model? Maybe somebody like Jessica Fletcher from *Murder, She Wrote* on TV. Face it. They were much more alike--they both lived in small coastal towns and had normal lives until people started dying. Yeah, she'd have to see if there were any old episodes available on Netflix. She needed a new role model.

Once Julie was no longer comparing herself to Kinsey, she flew through the book. Eleanor said this was the first Grafton book the club had read as a group. Since it sounded like most of the members were about the same age, she wondered if some of the other women had made the same discovery about Kinsey. Of course, she could read Agatha Christie's Miss Marple series, she laughed to herself. But somehow, Miss Marple was a little too old, a little too British, and too old-fashioned for Julie to identify with.

After completing two-thirds of the book, Julie looked at her watch and realized she had just enough time to feed Sheba and get ready to go to dinner. Sheba was snoozing in the sun in the armchair but quickly joined Julie as she headed downstairs.

After parking the car, she and Ted strolled down the street in Old Town. Looking around, she realized how much her little cozy village resembled Jessica Fletcher's Cabot Cove--the old buildings from the eighteen hundreds along with the newer ones made to look like they were vintage and the fishing boats at the wharf. Yes, she was going to try to behave more like Jessica Fletcher as she pursued this murder.

"What, Ted? Sorry, I was just looking at this quaint little town. Don't you love it? What were you saying?" Julie asked.

"I said I had to leave a voice message for Bill. He wasn't in. So I don't know if we'll get an update today or not."

"Well, I'm sure he'll call when he knows something," Julie said. *Or has something he wants us to know,* she thought.

They sat at a window table in the restaurant eating a great salmon with Caesar salad and crunchy french bread. The sun was still out. Days were long this time of year this far north. It would be close to ten before the sun finally set. Meanwhile at eight, the glow reflected on the river and the bridge was beautiful.

Chapter Eighteen

When she came downstairs the next morning, Ted was on his cell. It sounded like he was arguing with someone.

"They can't do that to me. I'm innocent. Please do something. I can't live in that jail."

Julie paused, staring at him. Ted looked terrified. His face looked gray with fear. She noticed that he was continuing to lose weight, and he slumped, looking at least fifteen years older.

After he hung up, she asked, "What's going on?"

"I have to turn myself in, Jules. That was Don. The DA's decided I'm the person they're going to prosecute for Tina's murder. They're arresting me. I probably won't be eligible for bail. I'm considered dangerous. Me? Can you believe it? Don said he'll try to get me out on bail, but not to count on it. Will you go in with me?"

"Sure. God, I can't believe this. How soon do we have to go? Do you want breakfast first?"

"Not me, I couldn't eat a thing. But go ahead. I have to be there at eleven. I'm going to be locked up with murderers and thugs. This is terrible."

"Well, they believe you're a murderer. Of course that's where they'll put you. Did Don give you any advice?"

"He told me there wasn't much he could do, but he'd try to figure something out. I can't do this."

"Maybe it's just for a day or two. I'm so sorry," she said, and she realized she meant it. While she wanted her house back, she hadn't wanted it back with Ted in prison. And she really believed he was innocent. She wondered if there was any new evidence.

"Did the police find anything more?" she asked.

"Not that we're aware of. Rather than arrest me here, they told me to report to the jail. Don thinks they need to make the case and look like they're actively prosecuting me. I'm really scared."

"I know you are," she replied. "I'll call Bill when I get back home and see what he has to say. Maybe he can do something."

They decided that Ted would take his car to the condo, and she would pick him up there. When Ted got into her car in the parking garage, he began to fidget. He bounced his hands on his knees all the way across the city, making her nervous. Once they got to the facility, there wasn't much she could do. They chatted with Don, she hugged Ted good-by, and watched the officers take him through the door. Don said she might as well go home.

When Julie returned that afternoon, the house seemed so empty without Ted. Even Sheba, who he'd ignored most of the time, seemed to notice he was gone. She rubbed against Julie's legs to show her love.

Julie realized that while Ted was a nuisance, it'd been comforting to have him around with all this talk of thugs and violence, just for company, if not for protection. She also thought about how easily they'd gotten back into their old routines of cooking together. *Enough,* she told herself. She was on her own again, just like she wanted to be. But she needed to see this murder solved, put closure on it.

What would Jessica Fletcher do? she questioned herself as she sat up in her crow's nest and pulled out a pen and paper.

First, talk to Bill. Even though he may not be who he says he is, he holds the keys to more information than anyone else at present.

Second, let Phil and Jon know I'm alone and ask them to be even more vigilant about looking for strangers around here.

Third, go to the condo.

She still had a key. Ted may not have known what to look for. She wanted to do a thorough search of the place. She'd do that tomorrow after the alarm people finished. But for now she could call Bill.

The phone rang just as she was ready to call. Bill was on the line.

"Hi," he said. "Just learned about Ted. So sorry. How about we go out to dinner tonight and catch up on the case afterwards at your place? I'll pick you up at six, if that's okay with you."

Dinner first. That sounded like a date. Was it? Was she still interested in Bill? As she chose her newer jeans and sweater to wear to dinner, she realized that of course she was interested. She'd been interested in him ever since she first met him. She just wasn't completely sure he was trustworthy.

Bill took her to the most extravagant restaurant in town--a delightful bistro with great ambiance, soft candles, linen tablecloths, and a mellow jazz duo--a pianist with a female vocalist. It was very romantic. And if he hadn't also been dressed in jeans and a sweater, she would've been concerned that she'd underdressed. But looking around, she noticed that most of the women were in casual clothes, so she fit right in.

They enjoyed martinis and an appetizer before the main courses arrived. Bill was easy to talk with. They discussed books, several favorites they'd both read including the current popular Stieg Larrson books. They held similar political views. Both voted for the president but wanted change more quickly than promised. And they both thoroughly enjoyed the jazz standards being performed for them.

It was a lovely evening; it would have been perfect if only they didn't have murder to discuss.

When Bill brought her home and came in, she made coffee to keep them clear-headed during their discussion. They'd decided they'd have an after dinner drink when they'd exhausted their conversation about Ted, the murder, and the current potential suspects.

* * * * * * * * *

When Julie awoke in the morning, it wasn't Sheba staring at her. Bill was smiling at her with a self-satisfactory grin on his face.

"Hello beautiful," he said.

"Hello," she responded. So she hadn't been dreaming as she remembered that the night had moved much faster than she'd planned. She hadn't even poured the coffee when Bill was behind her nuzzling her neck and turning her around to face him. God, she'd wanted him. And he'd seemed to want her. They were in her bed ten minutes later with all thoughts of Ted long gone from her mind, and she was pretty sure Bill's mind as well. She hadn't felt so alive and desired in years. What had she done? *Am I sleeping with the enemy?* she wondered. But Bill didn't seem frightening as she looked at him now.

He was staring at her with those fathomless eyes. He looked so appreciative of her, and she felt so beautiful, she almost purred like Sheba.

"I haven't felt like this in years," she said to him sitting up. "What a wonderful night. But I feel like I've betrayed Ted. Oh, not sexually," she added when he looked at her quizzically, "but because we did not discuss his case once all night."

"I don't see a problem," Bill responded. "I've got all day. How about you?" And he reached for her, pulling her back down on the bed.

"Bill, if we start this, we may never get focused on Ted. We've got to deal with his problems and see what we can do to get him out of jail. Let's get dressed and talk."

"Can't we talk without getting dressed?" he suggested.

"I'm afraid I wouldn't be focused," she answered.

"Ah, well, neither would I," he admitted.

While they ate breakfast, Bill told her that apparently the police had no real information. Reggie, Tina's ex, had an alibi at the gym, which Bill planned to check out. The police had no other suspects, and the DA's office was getting pressure to get this case to trial. So Ted was the suspect--he and Tina had argued, and he had no alibi.

"Did he ever tell you what they argued about?" Bill asked.

"Oh, just over weekend plans. Tina wanted to go away for the weekend. Ted said he didn't have the time. Apparently she had a tantrum, not the first, according to Ted and the police. So he took off for awhile to cool down. No big deal if he's telling the truth, which I think he is."

"Actually," Bill said. "I do, too. There's something bigger going on and he got caught up in it."

"I decided to go into the condo later today," Julie said. "After the alarm company's finished. I want to look around. Ted may not have known what to search for. I think it wouldn't hurt."

"Neither do I," Bill said. "Would you like me to go with you? I'd feel you were safer if I were there, too."

"Sure," Julie replied, relieved. She hadn't been back inside the condo since Tina had died, and although she didn't believe in ghosts, she really didn't want to be there on her own.

Chapter Nineteen

The alarm company was there promptly at ten and took several hours to complete their work. When they finished, she and Bill took off for the condo. As he drove into the parking garage, Julie felt a chill. She still hated this garage--actually she hated parking garages in general. She'd seen too many movies where people were attacked in them, and it'd always freaked her out. But since Vic had kidnapped her, her fears were much greater. *No parking garages at the beach,* she thought. Here her imagination easily went into fast forward. If by herself, she would've made a dash for the elevator. Again, she was glad Bill was with her.

They got in the the elevator. She pushed the buttons to the penthouse.

"It's supposed to have been cleaned up since the murder. Hopefully we won't see any blood or anything," she told Bill.

"I'm sure it's fine," he replied.

She knew her foreboding was more than just the fear of the residue from the murder. She'd hated this place--so sleek, so cold, so not her. And, she realized, she'd hated it more once Tina moved in. But then she'd thought she would never have to see it again.

She unlocked the door, and Bill followed her in. The shades were partially drawn, so it was dark. She shivered. The glass and mirrors looked cold to the touch, like ice. The metal surfaces, although clean and minimalist, felt unwelcoming. She shook again.

Looking at her, Bill put his arm around her for a moment, while he surveyed their surroundings.

"Wow!" Bill said. "This is really something. Look at the great new art on the wall."

She checked out the two huge abstracts hanging in front of them. Yes, they were new. Very avant-garde, painted by an extremely famous artist, she was sure, but they did nothing to soothe her. The brush strokes reminded her of exclamation points, blood-red slashes on the canvas.

Bill looked at her with sympathy and said, "It's not my style either. And it doesn't seem like yours from what I've seen at your beach house, but it is great art."

And Julie realized she had no idea what Bill's style was. She'd never been to his place. That was odd, now that she thought about it. Maybe now he would invite her over, now that they were sleeping together.

"No, definitely not my style," she said. "Although I lived with art like it for most of my married years. Let's get going. I just want to see if there's anything here at all."

She crossed in front of the black leather sofa, sat down, and moved the few items on the glass and metal coffee table. She wondered how furniture could make you feel depressed. But this room did. Not only now, but also sad about the life she'd lived in this unwelcoming space.

"No place to hide anything here," she said. "Why don't you check the media cabinets, and I'll look in the bedroom."

She deeply inhaled as she entered her former bedroom. Even the air felt heavy in here. Of course nobody had been here for awhile. But it was more than just stale air. She breathed doom and loss with every breath. God, she wanted out of here. But she continued her search knowing that the sooner they finished their looking, the sooner she could leave, hopefully for the very last time.

It was weird going through Tina's dresser drawers, her closet, knowing she was touching the belongings of someone who'd been alive a little over a week ago and whose possessions filled the drawers and closets where her own things used to be.

"Stop it," she told herself softly. "Just keep looking."

All she found were clothes, shoes, perfumes, cosmetics. When she pulled the shoeboxes out from the closet, she noticed a strange board wedged behind one of the boxes. It looked like it was supposed to fit tightly but had loosened. Maybe the police had not pushed it back when they'd looked around. Surely they would've taken the shoeboxes out. But no, she pulled the board free, and there was a tiny leather notebook.

"Bill," she called. "I think I found something."

"Coming," he replied.

She sat on the closet floor with the notebook. When he joined her, she opened it up.

"Nothing but numbers," she said. "Maybe dates? What do you suppose it means?"

She handed the notebook to him. Looking at it, he said, "I'm not sure. Could be some kind of code, or a list of dates and/or items. Let's take it with us."

He gave it back to her, and she put it in her pocket.

Julie returned the boxes to the closet, spent more time looking through both master baths, but found nothing else that seemed to be unusual.

Bill had found a couple of CDs in unmarked cases that he decided might be worth looking at. He volunteered to tackle the kitchen, much to her relief, while she scoured the home office. Neither of them found anything else of interest.

At last they could leave.

As she stepped out of the elevator, she took a large gulp of air. She finally could breathe again, even if it was the exhaust scented air of the parking garage. She climbed into the truck next to Bill and was grateful to be just a passenger headed back to the beach, to her crow's nest.

When Bill dropped her off, she gave him the notebook so he could study it. He hugged her good-by, gave her a kiss, and said he'd call later.

She greeted Sheba and climbed up to her nest. As she stretched out on the couch, she thought about her night with Bill. He seemed to be someone who truly cared about her, and she needed to be able to trust him. Maybe she was just allowing Ted's betrayal to confuse her. She'd slept with Bill, for god's sake. She certainly hoped she could depend on him. What a lovely night it had been.

She wondered how his decoding would go with the notebook, and what it might mean. Would it help Ted? She certainly hoped so. This was dragging on too long. As she nodded off, numbers in strange patterns began flashing in her mind.

Awakening about an hour later, she felt anything but rested. Numbers, she assumed from the notebook, had flipped through her dreams like the giant playing cards in *Alice in Wonderland.* What could they possibly mean? Would Bill even tell her? Would Bill want to see her again? What was she to him at this point?

Time to get moving, she thought. She decided a beach walk was just what she needed to clear her head, even if it was blowing a small gale. She bundled up in a big jacket, scarf, and hat, and headed over the dunes. The salty air was refreshing. She took off down the beach, one of only a very few people on the sand. The others were flying brightly colored kites. How cheerful they looked--their brilliant designs bobbing in the flurry.

She turned back toward her home. With her head down walking into the wind, she almost bumped into a man. She looked up to apologize and froze. This could be Vic's double, if it wasn't Vic himself. Shit. She'd just about convinced herself he was dead. It was hard to tell who he was since he was also wearing a jacket, hat, and scarf with large dark glasses covering his eyes.

"Sorry," she said, quickly moving forward.

"Not so fast, little lady," he replied, grabbing her wrist. "I think we have somethin' to talk about. You have somethin' of mine, and I want it back."

"What could I possibly have of yours?" she asked, struggling to get free.

He pulled her arm back behind her, which immediately stopped the struggle. The pain was intense.

"Ow!" she cried. "Why are you doing this?"

"Let's try this again," Vic said. "I want that notebook, and I want it now."

Well, at least she figured he didn't work for Bill. If he had, he would've known that Bill had the notebook.

"I don't know what you're talking about," she insisted.

"We know that you found somethin' in the condo. We heard you talkin' to your boyfriend in the parkin' garage. Now give it over."

"I, we, uh, gave it to the police already," she said.

"No, you didn't. You've been under surveillance. You haven't seen a cop since you left the condo. Now, we're goin' to walk back to your house, and you're goin' to get it for me. Understand?"

"Uh, yeah," she agreed, hoping that Bill's security guard would see them.

Chapter Twenty

Vic turned her around and put his arm around her tightly, as if she were his girlfriend. He was a huge man, and there was no escaping his grasp.

As they walked over the dunes, she scanned the area around her house, but saw no one. Of course, she had yet to spot one of Bill's bodyguards, so hopefully that was a good sign, and the guard was observing them. They approached the backdoor, and Vic stared as she entered the code to unlock the patio door. *Damn,* she thought. So much for her expensive new security system. However, if she managed to get out of this alive, she guessed she could reset the code. Where was that damn bodyguard?

As she hit the final number in the code and the green light came on, she prayed the bodyguard would show and turned her head to look.

"He's not here," Vic announced. "No point lookin'."

Vic was insistent that they go in. She didn't want to be alone in the house with him but could think of no delaying tactic. He opened the door, pushed her inside, and slammed the patio door quickly behind them, locking it.

"Now be a good girl," he said. "Give me the notebook."

Julie'd had enough. Jessica Fletcher she wasn't. She began to cry. "I don't have it," she finally said, realizing that now he'd have no excuse not to kill her.

"Where is it? At your boyfriend's? Well somebody's already there. One way or another, we're gettin' that notebook."

"What does it mean?" Julie asked, getting angry. "If it's worth killing for, what in the hell is in that notebook?"

"Information," he answered, "just information."

"Of what?" she asked, but he ignored her.

He led her to the dining room table, sat her down in a chair, and tied her hands behind her, fastening them to the chair back. She wasn't going anywhere soon. So far he hadn't flashed a gun. Maybe he wouldn't kill her after all.

Vic pulled out a cell phone and dialed someone.

"Yeah, I got her. She says it's not here. Did you get it? He wasn't there? You couldn't get in? What the hell do we do now? I'm probably dead meat if I try to leave; I'm afraid the cops could show?"

"I won't call the cops," Julie said, thinking that at least Bill wasn't home. If they hadn't found the notebook, maybe they'd have a reason to keep them both alive.

"Of course you won't, bitch," Vic said. "But your bodyguard might come back."

He listened intently to the person on the other end of the phone.

"Gotcha. Okay." He hung up.

"Well, we gotta go for a ride," he said, untying her hands from the chair back, but quickly retying them again behind her back. She was cuffed again. This was getting old.

"Let's go to your car," he said. "Where're your keys?"

She nodded. He saw them on the counter and picked them up, holding her with one hand. "Now, we're goin' to go into your garage, get into the car, open the garage door, and we're outta here. When we get in the car, I'll undo your hands. You'll drive, but my gun will be aimed at you. Understand?"

She nodded. So he did have a gun. What did she expect? This was getting worse. He could take her anywhere. Much easier to dispose of her someplace else, like the mountains where they were once before. Where was Bill? And where was his security? Hopefully they'd be able to help.

But if not, what could she do? Wasn't there something? Julie tried to think like Jessica Fletcher, but no brainstorms were occurring. She felt helpless, and she hated that.

Julie's phone rang just as they were walking toward the garage. Vic looked at it, saw who made the call, and picked it up, holding her with one hand.

"It's your boyfriend," he said. "We need him. Now you're gonna talk to him, tell him you'll meet him, here, but he must come alone, no one else, no weapons, and with the notebook. Understand?"

Julie nodded, swallowing hard. Vic held the phone up to her ear.

"Hi Bill," she said.

"Listen, I know what's going on. Security contacted me. The guard was afraid to make a move in case Vic was armed. He didn't want you hurt."

"Uh, Bill. I need you to come here, no weapon, no one else, and with the notebook," she said.

"I understand. I've been running errands. It'll take me a few minutes to get there. Tell Vic that. In fact, let me talk to him."

"He's on his way back from some errands," she told Vic. "He wants to talk to you."

As Vic put the phone to his ear, the keys fell to the floor. When he bent to pick them up, the gun dropped out of his holster. He had to release Julie to pick it up. It was almost funny, like a comedy routine. She almost laughed.

"Dammit," he muttered.

Julie saw her chance and ran for the front door.

"Stop," he yelled, as he fumbled for the gun on the floor and dropped the phone. "Shit," he said. He didn't move too quickly--that was the downfall of his huge size.

Julie managed to run, turning around quickly, so she could open the front door from behind. She made a dash outside, scurrying through her front yard as fast as she could with her hands tied behind her. Just as she ran through the open gate in the picket fence, she heard the door slam. Vic was after her. She wouldn't be able to outrun him for long with her hands tied.

She headed down the street, dodging a parked car. Vic was coming closer; she had to do something. If only she could untie her hands. God, she hoped he wouldn't shoot her. There was nowhere to hide.

She glanced over her shoulder. Vic was gaining on her. But then she saw Jon's Subaru pull out of his driveway and come toward her. He motioned her to get into passenger seat as he paused briefly, reached over, and opened the door. Julie rolled half onto the seat and the floor, and he took off with the door still open.

"A little excitement at your place?" he asked, as he reached across her to close the door, and floored the accelerator. They sped away leaving Vic behind.

"Where to?"

"Not sure," she replied, trying to catch her breath. "Just away from that awful man and here."

"Let's head downtown where there're lots of people. We can go into a busy cafe. You can call the sheriff. I don't think that thug will try to bother us there." He checked his rearview mirror and pulled to the side of the road. "No one seems to be behind us. Let me untie you." He reached around to undo her hands. Then he gave her his cell phone and resumed driving.

Julie breathed slowly, took the phone, and dialed 911. She tried to explain all that had happened, but finally quit, just saying, "There's a thug after me who broke into my house. I know he has a gun. A friend rescued me. We're in a blue Subaru Outback and are heading for downtown. We figured we're safer downtown around lots of people. We'll be at the Mexican food restaurant on the bay front, Josie's."

She listened, explained that this was related to the Tina Randall murder in the city, suggested they call Detective Gallagher, and hung up, exhaling deeply.

"You okay?" Jon asked.

"I think so," she responded. "Wow, you really pulled off a great rescue? Weren't you frightened?"

"Not really," Jon answered. "I was just heading to the grocery story when I saw that bruiser coming out your front door. Then I saw you running awkwardly with your hands behind you. So I tried to help. You said he had a gun when you talked to 911? It's a good thing I didn't know that." He laughed nervously.

"Well, anyway, you're certainly brave. It worked. Now I need to make another call," she said, dialing Bill's cellphone.

"Jon rescued me," Julie told him when he answered. "Someone may still be waiting for you at your house, so don't go home."

"Thanks, I won't," he answered. "Have you called the police?"

"We called the sheriff. Who knows how long it will take them to meet us. I also told them they could contact Gallagher for more information. We're going down to Josie's restaurant in old town. Can you meet us there?"

"I'll meet you there after the sheriff leaves. I don't want them to know that I'm involved so that I can keep investigating without interference. Glad you're safe. Can't believe that security didn't do a better job. You're a trooper, honey. So glad you're okay."

Honey, he called me honey, she thought. *He cares about me.* Then she looked around. No one seemed to be tailing them yet, but it was hard to tell as they'd gotten into the Friday late afternoon line of cars looking for parking in old town.

"We're lucky!" Jon cried. "Look, a car pulling out right in front of us, just a few doors down from the restaurant." And he maneuvered into the spot.

Julie handed him his phone, thanked him again for rescuing her, and said, "The Margaritas are on me." Then she realized she had no purse, no money, no credit cards. "Oops, they will be on me once I get some cash. Can you float me a loan?"

"Sure," Jon answered.

As they sat down in the crowded restaurant, he asked, "Who was the second call to?" Julie wasn't sure how to answer. However, if Bill was going to meet them there, then he'd figure it out anyhow.

Chapter Twenty-One

Julie was saved from answering by the prompt waiter who took their Margarita orders. Then the sheriff's deputies arrived and began to ask questions. It took quite a bit of time to give them a full report and the background data on the case. Finally, after the deputies left, Bill showed up.

"Hey, there," Bill said. "Started drinking without me, huh?"

Jon, apparently realizing now who Julie had called, said, "Welcome, Bill. Let's get the waiter back," and he waved to the waiter, giving a nod for another Margarita.

Julie and Jon were both eager to share information with Bill and to tell him what had taken place. Jon then excused himself from the noisy table, probably to call Phil, and to let him know what was happening.

While Jon was gone, Julie asked Bill about the notebook.

"No luck so far in decoding it. But we're working on it."

She wondered who "we" were, but didn't ask. Bill would probably answer "an associate," but she wondered if it weren't the FBI or some such group.

"I appreciated your letting me know that those thugs were also trying to get into my house, although security had notified me," he said. "How are you doing? Your situation sure sounded scary. Good thing Jon happened to notice."

"Well," she responded. "Actually, I'd asked them to help keep an eye on things since Tina's murder. I really didn't feel totally secure. What happened to your guard?"

"The guy took a leak. Said he was only gone a few minutes. He arrived back just as Vic was taking you inside. He stayed in the back trying to find a window to get in. He didn't want to alarm Vic because he was pretty sure he would be armed. He never thought Vic would take off out the front. I don't know what he was really thinking. We've got two guys on your house now, front and back."

Jon returned to the table. "Phil says there's been some activity around your house. He's not sure who's who, but I told him to come on down and join us for dinner. I hope that was all right."

"All right? That's great. Remember this goes on my tab, once I get my purse back from my house," Julie said. "You saved the day, Jon."

Jon blushed. "I just did what any good friend would do for another. I'm sure glad that you're okay, Julie."

When Phil walked in, they waved him over, ordered more Margaritas and some dinner. What a relief it was to be with friends, Julie thought. Then, glancing at Bill, she wondered, *just friends with benefits or is it something more?* It was hard to read him, and of course, they hadn't really been alone since everything had happened that afternoon.

After dinner, Jon and Phil headed for home, still jabbering about the excitement. Bill looked at Julie, pushed her hair off her forehead, and said, "I'm really glad you're okay. I don't know what I would've done if Vic had harmed you. Good thinking on your part to get out of there. Who knows what Vic would've done. What shall we do about tonight? Do you feel comfortable coming to my house?"

Comfortable? she thought. She couldn't think of any place she'd rather be.

"Can we stop by my place, feed the cat, and let me pick up a few things? I think everyone will probably be gone. In fact, I could probably stay there," she added, but not really wanting to.

"No," Bill replied. "That's out of the question.You're not staying there alone. We'll go by so you can get some stuff and take care of the cat. Then we'll go to my house. I have more security than you do--permanent security." He raised his eyebrows. "Also, let's see if we can find out anything more about the notebook. You said that Vic only mentioned information?"

"That's what he said. But he didn't say about what."

"I think we'll be able to figure this out," he said. "I still believe it's related to what took place in New Jersey before Tina came out here. Wish we knew what was in the box Vic took. That'd sure help us."

Bill came in with Julie when they got to her house. She packed a few things, fed a meowing Sheba, and checked her answering machine. Several messages. One from Eleanor asking about the excitement. She could call her later. One from the facility where Ted was, and it wasn't Ted. She listened carefully.

"This message is for Julie Maxwell. We need you to call regarding Ted Larson" and gave the return number and extension. She dialed quickly.

"This is Julie Maxwell," she said. " I'm returning your call about Ted Larson."

"We're sorry to inform you that Ted Larson has been moved to Memorial Hospital under security because of a knife attack. He's not allowed any visitors presently since he's still under arrest. His condition is serious."

"Oh my god!" Julie said, not believing that Ted had really been stabbed in jail. Was it just a routine stabbing, she wondered, or was someone trying to silence him? "Can I see him tomorrow?"

"That will depend on his condition. If he's better, his attorney will be allowed to see him and possibly you. We can't tell you that tonight. Please call our office tomorrow after nine. As his wife, you can contact the hospital for updates on his condition."

"Thank you," Julie answered.

"Bill," Julie said as she hung up. "Ted's been stabbed, and he's in the hospital. Do you think it's related to his case?"

"What? Stabbed? My guess is yes. If he were killed now, he's the person considered the murderer. The DA's office might not look any further for Tina's killer. Come on. Get your stuff. Let's go to my house."

As they pulled into his driveway, Julie realized that Bill lived less than a mile away from her. Positioned in the dunes above the beach sat his secluded, recently built, large Cape Cod style home.

"Wow! What a beautiful home," Julie said, admiring the steeply pitched roofline, the lovely front porch, the grey siding. "It looks like it belongs in Massachusetts."

"I'm pleased with it," Bill replied, smiling. "I think you'll like the inside, too."

He parked his truck in the garage, and they entered from the garage to the house, through a mud-laundry room, much like hers.

But there the similarity stopped. His home had a truly nautical theme--lots of red, white, and blue. His furniture appeared to be real antiques from the east coast, all adding to the Cape Cod charm.

"Let's take your stuff upstairs," he said, leading her to the huge master bedroom with a balcony and an endless view. "If you want to freshen up, the bath's in there." He pointed to the right.

Julie nodded. "Would you mind if I took a shower? I really feel I could use one."

"No problem," he answered, following her into the spa-like room. "However, you might want to soak in the jacuzzi tub instead. The guest towels are in that blue chest. Help yourself to whatever you need. There's a terry robe you can use hanging on the hook."

"Oh, yes," she replied, taking in the soothing ocean hues of the room accented by the beach glass colored tile. The tub was big enough for two, but she needed to be alone.

Bill, seeming to sense her mood, said, "Enjoy. I'm going downstairs. Call out if you need anything, and have a wonderful soak." He leaned over, kissed her, and left, pulling the door closed behind him.

After starting the water in the jacuzzi, Julie pulled off her sweat-soaked clothes and climbed into the over-sized tub. She turned the jets on and slid down into the water until only her head remained dry. She slowly relaxed as she watched the sun begin to set over the ocean while the massage of the water soothed her muscles and her mind. When she closed her eyes, she felt her heart slow down as the pulsing hot water did its work. God, she'd been on an adrenaline high for hours.

Julie dozed until the nearly tepid water awakened her. Sighing, she climbed out of the tub. Lazily, she dried off, the plush aqua towel softly buffing her skin, and then she snuggled into the comfy warmth of the matching terry robe.

As she descended the stairs, she felt renewed, as if she were years younger. Entering the dimly lit living room, she saw the blazing fire in the big stone fireplace and candles flickering on the mantle, the coffee table, and the windowsills. It was cozy and seductive--like a scene in a romantic movie.

Bill motioned her to the couch in front of the fire and poured her a Cognac. He then joined her, putting his arm around her shoulders. She snuggled against him as she sipped from the snifter--the Cognac warming her insides.

"I know you want some answers," he said gently, pulling her out of her reverie.

"Yes, of course I do," Julie replied, straightening up and turning to look him in the face, squaring her shoulders to hear what he had to say.

"While you were bathing, I called my contacts. They're still trying to decode the notebook. They thought it was related to some jewel heists, drug deals, and two murders that took place before Tina left. However, the dates don't correspond, if they are dates. We're still working on the rest of the information. We're not sure how valuable the notebook really is with Tina dead. She was necessary as both the eyewitness and the interpreter of her notes. We're beginning to believe that she may have been part of the mob, participated in some of the crimes, and got scared when she witnessed one murder. Still not sure."

"Will this get Ted off the hook, if he lives, I mean?"

"Possibly," Bill responded, looking her directly in the eyes and placing his arms around her shoulders. "Listen, are you still involved with him? Do you want him back? Because I can back off now if he's still part of your life."

"Oh," Julie answered. "He's part of my life all right, but not in the way you mean. Our relationship is over. I just want to help the poor guy get through this." Reaching up, she took his hand, interlacing her fingers in his. "I'm much more interested in you."

"And I think I'm becoming very interested in you," Bill said, wrapping her in his arms and kissing her.

He didn't rush her. He held her closely, kissing her slowly, then more passionately. All fear of who he might be left her as she looked into those blue eyes so focused on her. She'd never felt so beautiful, so cherished. *This is what it feels like to be truly loved,* she thought.

Chapter Twenty-Two

Julie was spent, warm, and satisfied. She could have slept serenely in Bill's arms all night. As she looked lovingly at him, he smiled contentedly. However, even in this bliss, Ted was present again.

Bill seemed to read her mind. "Hey, I know. It's okay. Go ahead and call the hospital."

And he was so understanding.

Julie called the hospital several times during the night. No new information on Ted's condition. When she called in the morning, they had some good news. He was definitely going to make it, and he would like her to come visit. Don had taken care of getting an okay for her to come in.

"Good news," she said. "Ted's out of intensive care and is going to be okay. I can go visit him. So, I think I'll get dressed and go into town."

"Do you need me to go with you?" he asked.

"No. If you'll just drive me back to my house so I can get my car, I'd appreciate that," Julie replied.

"Sure thing. But I'd be happy to go in with you if you wanted me to."

"Bill," she said, kissing him. "I'm really grateful for the offer, but I'm sure there are a zillion things you could do here, including working on the case. I'm so eager to get this behind us and move forward." She gave him a long look.

"Well, sure. I understand completely," he said, hugging her. "Now go get dressed, and I'll drive you home. When we get there, would you like me to take a look around to make sure everything's okay?"

"Sure. That'd be great."

When they got to her house, Bill parked out on the street, and she let him in so they could look around. Everything looked in place.

"Oh, by the way," he said. "Here's the notebook back. I've made copies for my team."

She went up to the crow's nest and put it in the top drawer of her desk along with the phone that she'd never given to the cops. *Later,* she thought.

She headed downstairs. Bill walked her into the garage, kissed her good-by telling her to call if she needed him, and returned to his truck. She backed out and headed over the mountains noticing no one following in her rear view mirror. That felt good.

* * * * * * * * * *

At the hospital, she found Ted's room, guarded. She showed her ID, gave her purse to the guard, was patted down, and was finally let in. Ted was looking pretty chipper, better than she thought he would.

"Well," she laughed. "That's the hard way to get out of jail, isn't it?"

"While it's a relief to be out, I don't recommend the procedure. It really hurt. I never did see who stabbed me. I was minding my own business and suddenly was held tight with a knife in my ribs. I went down. That's the last I remember. Why would somebody want to get rid of me? I don't know anything."

"Are you sure, Ted? Tina might've said something that didn't connect at the time. And guess what?" she asked, as she went closer and whispered. "Bill and I found a notebook of hers hidden in the condo with lots of numbers. Bill's trying to decode it."

"Bill certainly has been a lot of help, hasn't he?" Ted asked somewhat sarcastically. "How much time are you spending with him?"

"That's really none of your business. More importantly, what's going to happen with you?"

"Well, now that I'm not going to die, they think I can be released from the hospital in a day or two. Oh, not back to the jail. Don's taken care of that. I can go home. I'll probably need someone to care for me. You'll do it, won't you?"

Inwardly Julie groaned while she said, "Of course, Ted. Of course. You should probably stay at the condo though, so you'll be close to medical help."

"Yeah, they don't want me to leave the city. I'm still not free, just under house arrest. I'll have to wear an ankle bracelet. Won't be allowed to leave the condo."

"Better than jail, anyway, isn't it? Listen, I'm going to head out now," she said, kissing him on the forehead. "Keep me posted. I'll help where I can."

She got into her car and decided to go straight home. She was going to have more than enough of the city while caring for Ted. Her thoughts were focused on what she'd need to bring with her to the city and not on her travel when she saw warning signs for roadwork ahead. Damn, just what she needed.

She slowed up thinking that it was odd the signs weren't set up on her way in. Maybe there'd been a wreck or something since then. She came to a stop in front of the man holding the sign. As she did so, another man threw a rock through her passenger window, breaking it. He reached in and unlocked the door. God, was she being kidnapped again? This was getting old. How could she convince them that she knew nothing?

The stranger with dark glasses jumped into the car. He wore a beanie pulled over his head and close around his face.

"What do you want with me?" she croaked, beginning to cry.

"Shut up," he said. "Just start driving." He showed his gun. "Just do what I say, and you'll be okay."

Sure I will, Julie thought. *What choice do I have?*

"Yes sir," she answered.

Looking around she realized that this time there'd be no one to rescue her. It was just Beanie Baby and herself. She wondered what was to be her destination.

"Turn this thing around. We're going back to the city. My boss wants to talk to you."

Your boss, she thought. She wondered who that was and what he thought she could possibly tell him. Of course, there was the notebook.

She also wondered when Bill would begin to miss her. And a small part of her questioned whether Bill wasn't just using her. *Don't think about that now,* she told herself. *Think about what you can do to save yourself.*

"You know," she said looking at the gas gauge. "We're going to have to get gas before too long."

"There're no stations on this whole road. If you had enough gas to get home, you've got enough to get where we're going."

"Well, just wanted to let you know it's low," she answered. "Didn't want to strand you somewhere."

"Shut up and drive," he said.

Jessica Fletcher, Jessica, Jessica, she thought trying to channel her. *What would you do? What would your screenwriters have you do?* That was silly. Jessica wouldn't ever be in this predicament. She didn't drive. Maybe that was the lesson Julie needed to learn from all this. Give up driving. Get a bicycle.

She was almost getting hysterical. *Slow down,* she told herself. *Think rationally. What can I do?*

First, she thought, she could have an accident. Drive in front of another car, hit something. She didn't want to hurt anyone else, but maybe there was something she could hit. She'd keep her eyes open for that.

Second, why not try bribery? It didn't work for Vic, but this was a different thug. Maybe he didn't get paid very much. She might try money.

Third, third, uh, she could try to make a run for it at a stop sign. Of course getting out of her seatbelt could prove difficult.

Fourth, maybe when they got into town, she could catch a red light, lay on the horn, and turn off the engine. Would he shoot her in front of pedestrians and other drivers? He might, but he might not. Of course, her luck would be that she wouldn't hit a single red light. Maybe she could just stop suddenly in the middle of downtown, if, of course, they were going into town.

"Uh, sir," she finally said. "Do you know what your boss wants with me? I can't understand how I can be helpful in anything?"

"Just drive," he said. "I don't have a clue. I just do what I'm told."

"How about we drive to my bank?" she asked. "I can get you a huge amount of money to let me go. I really can."

He looked at her incredulously. "You really think you can buy me off so the boss is after me like he's after you?" he said. "I don't think so."

"Well, I'd be happy to get you enough to get out of town."

"Out of town isn't nearly far enough. Now just shut up and keep driving."

They were leaving the mountains and entering the outskirts of the city. What would happen next? Would she be able to put any of her other plans to work? Would he kill her if she tried?

"Turn right at the next street," he said.

Shit. They were going into an industrial area on the edge of town. And since it was Saturday, hardly any other vehicles were around. Sounding the horn wasn't going to attract much attention out here.

He ordered her to make a few more turns, and finally, to pull into a secluded warehouse parking lot. This wasn't getting any better. She was grinding her teeth together she was so scared. Her hands began to shake as he used an electronic gadget to open one of the huge doors and told her to drive in. She had no choice. She drove in. The door thudded loudly behind her as it closed, locking her into a terrifying dark warehouse.

Chapter Twenty-Three

Now what? Julie thought. Beanie Baby just sat there, playing with his fingers, waiting.

"Aren't we going to get out?" she asked, wondering why she was in such a hurry.

"We'll wait until we're told," he replied. "Just sit still."

Although it wasn't that cold out, the dim light of the warehouse and her situation chilled her, and she shivered a little. "Could I get my jacket from the backseat?" she asked. "I'm freezing."

"Just stay put," he ordered, and reached back with one arm to retrieve it. "Here." He handed it to her.

"May I undo my seat belt to put it on?" she asked.

"Yeah, but no tricks. I heard you was a bit of a fast one. Funny you don't look like it."

Julie unhooked her seatbelt and was just putting the jacket on, when there was a crash behind them. Beanie Baby turned around to look back, and Julie opened the door, running with her jacket half off of her.

"Stop, bitch!" Beanie yelled.

God, she thought, *they all call me the same name. No originality whatsoever.* She laughed to herself. Why the hell was she laughing? *Snap out of it,* she told herself. *This is not the time to get hysterical.*

She'd run towards the closest door which, fortunately, was unlocked. She pulled it open and entered a huge factory sort of room with all kinds of equipment, catwalks, and vats. Was this some kind of brewery? It smelled like hops.

She hastily made a dash for the nearest vat and hid behind it. This spot allowed her to look around and see where she might go next. She wanted to avoid the catwalk as she'd always been fearful of heights, especially when you could see through the mesh-like floors to the bottom. So what did that leave?

The door opened behind her and slammed shut. She peeked around. Beanie had a friend with a shaved head and tattoos where most people had hair. He was huge, too. God, did all these guys work out at the gym? The only good thing was that so far none of these giant men moved real quickly. They were splitting up to look around. She was running out of choices.

Quickly she sprinted for the next vat. She moved from vat to vat until she was nearing the end of the building. She heard feet coming towards her but scarier still were the noises on the catwalk. One guy was up there, and he would be able to spot her with no problems. She had to get out.

She continued running from one vat to other equipment to another vat, and finally to the door. She opened it just as she heard Beanie Baby yell, "Stop. I see you. Stop or I'll shoot."

She slammed the door behind her. Now where was she? Some kind of storage warehouse with rows and rows of shelves. Maybe she could move some stuff around and hide behind the cartons on one of the shelves. They were wide enough. However, time wasn't on her side. Once she became immobile, all they had to do was a very controlled search, row by row, shelf by shelf, and they would find her. No, she couldn't stop. She had to keep going. There had to be a door to the outside. That was her only hope.

The door she'd entered opened again. They must both be in the room now. She darted quickly from one shelf to another as she made her way toward a red exit sign. Would they be smart enough to divide up and have one of them waiting for her there?

No time to worry. She had to keep moving. She was breathing hard but had just about made it to the door when she slipped on a spill on the floor. She couldn't regain her balance. Down she went, scraping her knee in the process.

Julie heard a yell. "There she is. By the door. Stop her."

She jumped to her feet, ignoring the pain in her knee. She had her hand on the door handle when she felt her jacket catch. Good god, someone had hold of her jacket. She was glad she'd never placed both arms into it. She pulled her left arm out. Her jacket slipped away as she opened the door and at last found herself outside.

Without thinking, Julie ran straight toward the first vehicle she saw and crouched behind it. Both men were running towards her. She couldn't rest, couldn't worry about her scraped knee. She just had to keep moving, weaving in and out of vehicles parked in this lot--most of which looked like equipment and trucks for the brewery.

As she rounded the next vehicle, she looked behind her and saw the men approaching. Glancing down, she noticed the key was in the ignition. Maybe she was about to get lucky. She hopped in and started the truck up. As she was backing out, a hand grabbed the driver's door handle.

No, you don't, she thought reaching over to lock the door, while flooring the accelerator. He held on for a moment, but she started going too fast. He couldn't keep his feet moving that quickly and had to let go or risk being dragged along. He let go.

Just in front of her was a locked gate. Too late now to slow down. Anyway, she didn't intend to stay in this vehicle yard. She gunned the engine some more, closed her eyes, and rammed the gate.

When she opened her eyes, she was back in the front parking lot. She got her bearings, drove past her car, and took off for the highway. Several turns later, she was back on the main road and heading into the city.

Enough was enough. Time to let the cops know what was going on. She drove straight to the police station. She parked the truck in the police department lot since it was too big for the street, grabbed the keys, and marched into the building while a voice behind her said, "Lady, you can't park that truck here. This lot's for employees only. Can't you read?"

"Can't you see how angry I am? You don't want to mess with me right now. I need to see a detective, and I need to see one right now. Get it?" She tossed him the keys. "Park it anywhere you want. I don't care. It's not mine anyway."

And with that, she marched into the building.

She approached the desk in the lobby saying, "I need to see Detective Gallagher immediately. It's urgent."

"Let me see if he's in," the receptionist answered. "Please have a seat."

"A seat? I said I need to see him right now, not in five minutes. Tell him I'm Julie Maxwell, and I was kidnapped."

"Yes, Ma'am," the receptionist said, picking up her phone and ringing him.

"Detective Gallagher, there's a Julie Maxwell here who says she was kidnapped. She wants to see you. You do? Okay. Will do."

She looked up a Julie. "He wants to see you in his office. Would you like me to show you where it is?" she began.

But Julie was already through the door, racing down the hall, halfway to his office. Gallagher was waiting for her outside his door.

"Well, Julie Maxwell. What's this all about?"

Julie began to explain.

"Come on in," he said. "Have a seat. I'm going to record you, if that's okay."

"Sure," she answered. She began to tell him about her most recent kidnapping.

"Just a minute," he said. "You seem to have a history with some of these guys. How about you tell me the whole story."

Not remembering what he knew or didn't know, she tried to retell the story from the very beginning. When she got into the break-in at Ted's office, she realized she should also let him know about Tina's telephone. Bill had told her to do that a long time ago. She'd never gotten around to it.

Gallagher yelled at her. "You mean you have evidence in a murder case? And you're just getting around to telling me about it? Lady, I could lock you up for withholding evidence. Where is that phone?"

"My house," she said, neglecting to tell him that Bill had seen it first. That would probably only make him angrier.

"I meant to tell you, but I forgot with all that has happened," she said.

"Yeah, right."

And she knew immediately that he didn't trust her. She really couldn't blame him. As she continued her story, she wondered whether she should tell him about the notebook. Bill had already copied the pages.

"Uh, I have another piece of possible evidence," she began.

Gallagher glared at her, took off his glasses, and thumped them on his desk. She assumed that thumping his glasses was his way of controlling his anger and not hitting the desk or her.

"Well," he began. "You gonna tell me?"

"Uh, I went to Ted's condo to look around and found a little notebook in the closet hidden behind a wedged board behind a shoe box. I assumed that the cops had seen it. It wasn't that well hidden. Anyway, it's nothing but numbers." Again, she didn't mention Bill, or the fact that he was with her this time, or that they had a clue what it might mean.

"Lady, I should lock you up for withholding evidence in a murder investigation. What do you think you're doing? Playing detective? Think you're a fuckin' little Nancy Drew?"

She blushed. He just didn't know that Nancy Drew had morphed into Jessica Fletcher. How embarrassing.

"I'm sorry, sir. I really wasn't trying to impede justice. A lot's happened to me." She finished the story.

"Yeah, a lot has happened to you. I'm sending a detective to get your car. He'll deliver it to your house. Meanwhile I'm driving you home to get that evidence. This is important stuff. We should've had it immediately."

God, he was probably going to scold her all the way home. Well, she'd just have to listen. She supposed she did deserve it.

First he called a patrol to check out the brewery. Then he phoned someone regarding her car and repeated where it was located. He told them to dust it for prints before driving it to her house. Gallagher told the officer he would meet him at Julie's house and give him a ride back to the station.

After hanging up, he nodded to Julie and stood up. "Okay, let's go," he said.

Chapter Twenty-Four

In an attempt to get back into Gallagher's good graces, Julie apologized for keeping him out so late on a Saturday.

"You probably have a wife and kids at home, and I'm making you late for dinner," she said.

He looked at her. "Wife and kids? Hard to keep those with the hours I work. I used to have a wife and kids." Then he looked at her again.

"You've had a long day, too," he said, more gently. "You eaten?"

Until he asked, Julie hadn't realized that she really hadn't eaten all day. She shook her head no.

"I haven't had dinner either," he said. "Let's stop and get something on the way out of town, shall we?"

They pulled into a typical diner that she associated with cops from TV shows. But the food was good and filling, and she was starving. She didn't have a purse. He treated. She was beginning to think a little better of him and could even see the situation from his point of view. She really was guilty of hiding evidence. And now he was being kind.

She looked at him more closely. He was about ten years her junior with a stocky build. He wore black-rimmed glasses over dark eyes. His hair was curly, cut shortish, but not too short. It looked like the kind of hair that made its own decisions. Unruly, you'd call it. When he wasn't angry, he listened like what she said was important. Julie felt she could trust him. But could she trust him enough to tell him about Bill?

Not yet, she thought. Maybe later, but not now. She didn't want to betray Bill just when he was beginning to get answers. Ted's life was at stake.

She thanked him again for dinner as they returned to his car. She dozed a little on the trip to the coast. The day had taken a lot out of her.

He woke her as he pulled into her driveway behind her Lexus. "You're home," he announced. "Glad the officer made it back with your car. He radioed that your purse and keys were still in it when he got to the lot. He said he would drive on out, and he would wait here until we arrived. There he is." He pointed to a man waiting in the front yard stretched out in her adirondack chair.

As they entered her house, she immediately knew someone had been there.

"Somebody's broken in," she said. "Look. Books are off the shelves, kitchen cupboard doors are open. I wonder what I'll find upstairs."

The other cop said, "Someone ran off as I pulled in. Since we don't have jurisdiction here, I radioed the sheriff. They didn't have a unit nearby, but I gave a description. Big guy, bald, scary looking. You know him?"

"That sounds like Vic or one of his friends," Julie said. "I hope they didn't get anything."

"Well, let's go up and see," said Gallagher.

Her bedroom had been pretty well ransacked. Clothes were strewn about, drawers opened and dumped, the bed torn apart. Julie was heartsick that her belongings had been so violated. The cottage that had felt so safe and secure felt more frightening as if the thug's presence lingered. She breathed deeply. She needed to get her life and home back.

She wondered it they'd taken her gun. She pulled her nightstand drawer from its tipped over position on the floor. Her revolver was lying there.

"Jesus Christ!" Gallagher said. "Our lady detective has a gun. That's scary."

"No, it's not," Julie replied. "I got it for protection, and I know how to use it."

"Sure you do," he said. "Sure you do."

"I do," she insisted. Then she told Gallagher about her dad and the shooting range.

"Okay, okay," he gave in. "I believe you. Now where did you put the other stuff?"

"Up in the crow's nest. I just hope the jerk didn't get up there. That's my sanctuary. I've never invited anyone up."

"Am I invited?" Gallagher asked sarcastically.

"I guess so," she answered, disappointed that a cop was her first crow's nest guest.

She breathed a sigh of relief as she stepped up into the nest. Apparently the guy was scared off by the policeman driving her car into the driveway before he made it up here. She went over to her desk, opened the drawer, and pulled out both Tina's cellphone and notebook. She handed them to Gallagher with another apology.

"At least they're still here," he said, taking them into his possession. "Now tell me again. What size was the box the guy took from Tina's office?"

Julie explained again that it looked like a box containing file folders.

"Well," he said. "Let's get back downstairs. I want to secure your house before I leave. I think now that they know the cops have been here, they'll assume that the evidence went with us. Hopefully they'll leave you alone. We don't have any jurisdiction here, but I'll call the sheriff and ask them to do extra patrols, if they can."

He looked at Julie again. "I know I was a little rough on you. But I hope you see my point. It's hard to solve a case without all the evidence available."

"I know. I'm sorry, too. I was just trying to help Ted. And thanks," she added. "Thanks for the ride and dinner. I really appreciate it."

He checked the windows and the doors and told her to lock up behind him. Which she promptly did.

After he left, she looked at the mess and decided it could wait until tomorrow. She quickly fed Sheba, eager to go upstairs.

She thought about calling Bill and letting him know what had happened. Part of her figured he probably knew most, if not all, of it as he seemed to have antennae everywhere. Another part of her still wasn't sure she could trust him completely. And the rest of her was too tired to care.

She took a quick shower, put on sweats, and retreated to her crow's nest, where she sat in the darkness watching a night-time sea reflecting a little bit of moonlight. She snuggled under the afghan she kept on the back of the couch, and drifted off to sleep. She was so exhausted she slept the night through.

As she opened her eyes, Sheba was there on the couch arm, staring at her, almost as if to ask: Why aren't you home very much? Who are these strange men who keep coming in? and When are you going to feed me?

She reached up to pet her, and Sheba began to purr, questions seemingly forgotten.

She got up, and they went downstairs together.

Julie spent the morning straightening up the mess in her house and ignoring her phone. The message machine was blinking like crazy, and she'd had more calls since she got up. She wasn't in the mood to talk to anybody. Instead she cranked up her stereo and sang along with several of her favorite vocalists while she tidied things up.

The phone she could ignore; the pounding at the door she couldn't. She looked out the window. Bill was standing there. God, she really didn't want to see him. But she was sure he could hear the music blasting and knew she was in the house.

Oh well, she thought. *Let's get it over with.*

"Hi Bill," she said opening the door.

"Julie, are you all right? I was so worried about you? What happened? My security guys said they were called away on a wild goose hunt--someone claiming to be you said she needed them. Then when they got back, they saw an unmarked cop car in the driveway behind your car and decided to lay low. What's going on?"

Julie invited him in, and he hugged her.

"I was so worried," he repeated.

"Come sit down," she said. "Let me get some coffee, and I'll tell you."

While she made the coffee, she decided to tell him the truth. The truth was so much simpler than omissions or lies, and he probably knew most of it anyway. Somehow he seemed to keep a pulse on everything. Except for the security guards not being there when her house was searched. And the security guard who didn't catch Vic. Yeah, there were some holes. But nothing she told him would really matter anyway.

"Well, Bill, yesterday was an intensely frightening and long day." She told him everything, pausing only when he commented saying, "You poor thing," or "I bet you were scared," and "You really stole their truck? Good for you." But other than that, he listened and nodded when she told him about giving the phone and notebook to the police.

"You should've given the phone to them much sooner like I suggested. But it's good they've got everything now. And you didn't mention my name?"

"No, I couldn't see what would be gained by adding your name to the list."

"Good girl," he said. "That allows me to remain free to continue our investigation without them breathing down my neck. You've done the right thing. I'm so sorry you had such a rough time of it."

He put his arms around her and held her tightly. It felt good to be in his embrace, so safe, and it would have been great to let him make love to her, but her upstairs was a mess. She knew she couldn't relax until she finished putting things away, getting those nasty vibes from those gangsters out of her home.

"Bill, thanks for being here for me," she said. "Let's get together later. Right now I've still got a major cleanup to do. I don't want to play until I've finished putting everything to rights. Do you understand?"

"Sure, I get it. No problem," he answered. "Let's get together for dinner tonight. I'll call you this afternoon. Okay?"

"Perfect," she answered, walking him to the door. "See you tonight."

He really was an understanding guy. Maybe too understanding? There it was again. That uncomfortable feeling she got when thinking about his involvement in all of this. What did he really want?

Chapter Twenty-Five

Fortunately, very little was broken in all the mess--a vase, a glass float, a couple of book spines damaged. Mostly it was just picking things up and putting them away. As she finished up several hours later, she thought about calling Eleanor. Eleanor seemed like the kind of person who could help her find someone to give a blessing to the house, smudge some sage, get the evil spirits out that had disrupted her peace. She'd planned to do that before as part of a house warming. But after the break-in, she really needed it soon.

After she apologized to Eleanor for being out of touch, she briefly explained the break-in and asked if Eleanor knew someone who could bless her house.

"I know exactly the right person--Reverend Susan, the minister at the Unitarian Universalist Society, does the most incredible rituals. Would you like me to call her? Maybe we could meet for coffee somewhere."

"Sounds good. Or you could bring her here for coffee, and she could see my house. Do let me know when you talk to her. I really appreciate it."

"Sorry you're having such a tough go of it," Eleanor said. "And you think it's all related to Tina's murder?"

"Must be. Can't think of anything else. Anyway, I really appreciate your friendship and help."

"Bye-bye. Will talk to you after I've spoken with Reverend Susan."

As she hung up the phone, she thought how lucky she was to have Eleanor as such a good friend, and so quickly, too. She glanced at her answering machine and realized she couldn't put off listening to the messages any longer.

Several calls were from Bill. She didn't need to return them since she had already talked to him in person. One was from Eleanor asking if she wanted to go to yoga yesterday. Another call she wouldn't have to answer. Two telemarketing calls.

The rest were repeat messages from Ted. He never was patient. He must have dialed every ten minutes for a couple of hours before he finally slowed down to once every hour. He was being released from the hospital on Monday. *That's tomorrow,* she thought. He needed her to meet him at the condo. The cops would deliver him there, put the bracelet on his ankle, and explain the whole procedure to him. He needed her help.

She called him back. "Hi Ted," she said.

"Where the hell've you been?" he yelled. "I've been trying to reach you for hours."

"Calm down. You've got me on the phone now." She threatened, "If you continue to yell at me, I'm hanging up."

"Okay, okay. Sorry. Can you meet me at the condo tomorrow afternoon? Also, can you pick up some groceries and stuff? Oh, and bring some clothes so you can stay there with me."

"What do you mean, stay there?" she asked.

"Well, you don't expect me to stay there alone, do you? I can't go anywhere, get groceries, or anything. Plus I was injured. I need you there, Jules."

"Let me think about it," she said. "But yes, I'll meet you there tomorrow. And I will get some food and things for you at the store. Anything in particular?"

As Ted gave her a list of what he wanted her to buy for him, she knew that most of the next day would be taken up shopping, meeting him at the condo, and getting him settled in. She would throw in a small suitcase, packed in case she did decide she needed to stay over.

As hard as this was on Ted, he really had no idea how difficult it was for her. She'd been loving her new life which seemed to have disappeared almost as suddenly as it had begun.

After Bill called confirming the time he'd pick her up for dinner, she went up to the crow's nest and read for an hour or so finishing her book. Kinsey had solved her case. Good for Kinsey. Now if only she could solve hers. She watched the fog swirl on the beach and lit her fireplace to take the chill out of the air. Finally she dozed for about half an hour in her chair. *This was more like it. Life at a slower pace.*

She showered and dressed in a warm sweater, jeans, and UGG boots. Good clothes for a chilly night, she thought. When the doorbell rang, she grabbed her fleece jacket, greeted Bill who looked as handsome as ever with that sun-bleached hair falling over those brilliant blue eyes, and followed him out to his truck. They were going to the Crab Cooker--the perfect place for a damp evening.

She and Bill didn't talk about the case once. He seemed to sense her mood, and they spent the evening talking about travel, books, and just getting to know one another better. The crab chowder and french bread were delicious, accompanied by a lovely white-blend house wine. She felt warm and relaxed as they sat by the wood stove in the cozy restaurant.

They finished the rest of the bottle of wine, then bundled up. Bill, too, liked to walk in the fog, so they took a leisurely stroll around the docks before trekking back to his truck. A lovely evening, she thought.

And it became lovelier still. Bill came in. Eventually they made their way to her bed where he softly made love to her, treating her with exquisite care, as if she were a treasure to be valued. Exactly what she needed after the week she'd had. They didn't talk but fell asleep in one another's arms. She felt cherished, cared for, and warm from the inside out. Life was perfect, for one night anyhow.

* * * * * * * * * *

When she woke up, she could hear kitchen noises. Bill must be cooking breakfast, she thought contentedly. As she came downstairs, the aroma of coffee, eggs, and pancakes wafted around her. She joined him at the table.

"I could get used to this," she said.

"So could I," he answered with a smile.

The fog had cleared, and it was a sunny day out.

"How about a walk on the beach?" she asked. "Before I drive into town and you go on home."

"Sure. After we finish eating, let me clean up in here while you get dressed for a walk."

They had a slow stroll on the beach, and he told her about a headlands north of them with a cove that could only be reached by walking along the coast. The cliffs were too steep and heavily forested to give access down. He told her she'd love it--great tide pools, interesting caves. She nodded. Perhaps later in the week, he'd suggested. She'd agreed.

When they got back to her house, he kissed her good-bye and left in his truck. She went inside, packed a small overnight bag, grabbed Ted's grocery list, and drove into the city. She shopped at the store near the condo, picking up the information for grocery delivery. That should take care of Ted's problems of not getting out later in the week. She'd stay one night, but hopefully that was it.

Arriving before Ted, she scurried through the parking garage, breathing a sigh of relief when the elevator door shut, and she was safely enclosed. When she walked into the penthouse, she looked around. *Deja vu*, she thought. The condo had been ransacked much like her cottage. This was getting so tiresome.

She called Gallagher who said he'd be over shortly. Some other officers were bringing Ted. They were on their way now.

Julie put the grocery bags down on the counter and began to cry. Her daily life was totally out of control. The craziness had to end soon. She couldn't keep going like this.

She heard the key in the door, wiped her eyes, and saw Ted enter with the two officers. He looked around.

"Christ, what happened here?" he bellowed.

"Looks like you've been the victim of a break-in like I was," she answered.

"You were? When?" Ted asked.

"It doesn't matter. Let's just deal with your bracelet. Gallagher's going to be here soon to look around. Then we can begin to pick things up."

When the officers heard Gallagher's name, it was apparent that they knew they didn't need to write a report. So, they spent the time explaining the bracelet procedure to Ted. They set up sensors. He wouldn't be allowed to go out his front door. He was literally caged in his own condo.

But it had to be better than a cell, Julie thought.

Gallagher arrived just as the officers were leaving. He walked around the condo with them. All the rooms had been searched and belongings were strewn everywhere.

"Are you aware of anything missing?" he asked them.

"It's too difficult to tell at this point," Ted answered. "But, no, I don't think so."

"Yeah, it looks like they were hunting for something," Gallagher said. "There's still something they want. I wonder if they found it. It's hard to tell."

Gallagher was efficient, Julie thought. He didn't waste time chatting, just wrote out a report and left wishing them happy housecleaning.

"Thanks," Julie responded. "I can't believe I'm doing this again." She realized that she was comforted knowing Gallagher was on her side or, at least, listening to them.

Julie and Ted divided up the condo to begin restoring order. She gave him the kitchen so he could also put the groceries away while returning items to cupboards and shelves. She reminded him to avoid putting things away on the really high or low shelves, so he wouldn't have to stretch so much where he was still stitched up. She didn't want him to re-injure himself. After he finished there, he could move on to his office.

She began in the living room which had the least damage, since it had the fewest hiding places. She then worked in the master bedroom and finally the two master bathrooms.

She started with Tina's bathroom. As she put the plastic bag with the rolls of toilet paper back under the sink, she remembered that she'd used toilet paper rolls as a hiding place when she was a child. She'd had a friend over. They'd played a game of hiding a small treasure, a ring, she thought. Anyway the rule was to hide it anywhere in Julie's bedroom or bath. Then they would shout warm or cold as the other person got closer or further. Her friend Kathy had never found the ring where she'd hidden it. She'd pulled out the bag with the bunch of toilet paper rolls in it, slipped the ring into the roll at the bottom, and then stacked all the other bags back into the plastic bag, and stored it back under the sink. It'd been a perfect spot for something small.

Maybe something small was hidden in one of these, she thought. She dumped the rolls onto the bathroom floor. Then she inspected each one before she placed it back in the bag. Voila. One roll had something taped inside. She reached in with a nail file and pried it loose.

Aha. A thumb drive. This is what they're looking for.

She slipped it into her jean's pocket and put everything back in order.

Chapter Twenty-Six

She decided not to mention the thumb drive to Ted. He had enough to worry about, and she needed to decide what to do with it. Before she did, however, she wanted to see what was on it.

Ted was just finishing up the two rooms he had tackled and joined her in the living room.

"What a day," he sighed. "Although it's good to be home. I'm so glad you're going to be staying with me, Jules. After all our work, instead of cooking, why don't we call for take-out?"

"Sounds good to me," she responded. This wasn't the time, she decided, to let him know she was only staying the one night.

They looked through the take-out and delivery menus they'd accumulated over the years and decided on a nearby Chinese restaurant. Ted called and ordered while Julie stretched out on the couch.

She looked up on the wall at the paintings she hated and briefly wondered how Bill knew they were new paintings. Then she realized that they were probably paintings the artist had just created and that's all he meant by new paintings. He would've had no way of knowing that Ted had recently acquired them. Or would he?

She was eager to get on the computer and check out the thumb drive. But Ted would ask questions. She'd have to do it later.

When the food arrived, they sat around the coffee table eating with chopsticks from the containers. Good dinner, and Ted had leftovers for another night.

Ted said he hadn't slept well in his hospital room and wanted to go to bed early. That worked for her. He offered her the bedroom, but she declined, saying she'd take the pull-out sofa in the study.

"Besides," she told him, "I have work to do on the computer."

"Oh, Jules, I'm so sorry for all this. I bet you've gotten behind with your real estate," he said. "Yes, please do use the computer. Make yourself at home."

Make myself at home, she thought. She'd never felt at home when she lived here and certainly didn't feel at home now.

"Thanks Ted," she answered. "Sleep well."

"Good night. And thanks again," he said.

She didn't think she'd ever heard him say thank you so many times. Maybe he was changing a little. Perhaps he'd come out of this whole thing a little less arrogant and demanding. Not that it would really matter to her. She didn't plan on spending time with him once this was over.

When he'd settled in for the night, she went to the computer. She really hadn't used a thumb drive before and hoped the process wouldn't be too difficult.

She found the right place to insert it and then turned the computer on. As she looked at the screen, she was flabbergasted at what she saw.

This wasn't about a Ponzi scheme. This was horrible--logs and photos of what looked like the child sex trade. It appeared to be an inventory of the children--when they arrived, dates, numbers assigned to them, and a photo of each. Jeez, some looked like they weren't much older than toddlers. This drive included an accounting of where they'd been sent, how much the dealer was paid. There were hundreds of listings on this one drive.

No wonder those thugs were after Tina and now, after Ted and her. This was totally damning information. She couldn't stand to see any more. The first part seemed to have ended three years ago when Tina disappeared. She looked again. There appeared to be some newer data--these might match the dates in the notebook through this spring. Good god, had Tina stumbled onto the same gang here?

Now, the question was who should she give it to? If she gave it to Gallagher, would it get Ted off the hook? Or would it be better to give it to Bill so he could use it in Ted's favor? Maybe she should make a copy for Bill and give the original to Gallagher.

She had no idea how to copy a thumb drive, but discovered she could copy the information to blank CDs without too much expertise needed. Ted always had a stash of those around. Sure enough, she found them and began copying the data onto the CDs. It took quite awhile and a number of CDs since the thumb drive held a ton more information.

At last she was done. She put the drive into her purse, and put the CDs on the shelf with the others. It was probably better to separate them in case anybody came looking again.

Ted had insisted on making up the sofa bed with her before he went off to his room. Now she was glad. She was exhausted. After a quick trip to the bathroom to brush her teeth and get ready for bed, she collapsed between the sheets, pulling the covers up over her head. If only she could make those images go away as quickly. It was heartbreaking to think of all those poor children. How could people be so evil? She was glad she didn't know people like that.

* * * * * * * * *

After breakfast, she told Ted she needed to make some business calls and excused herself to the study. First, she dialed Gallagher. He wasn't in. He had personal business to attend to, she was told, and would be out of the office all day and most of the next. She was asked if she would like to speak to someone else.

Julie decided that she would wait for Gallagher and just left her name and cell phone number asking him to call when he got a chance. She decided to wait and call Bill when she got home. She would rather tell him what she'd found in person.

Now Julie geared up for battle. She knew Ted would be angry that she was leaving, but she had things to do.

"Ted," she said. "I have to go back to the coast. I have business to attend to." She knew he would think it was real estate business.

"I understand," he said. "But you'll be back tonight, right? In time for dinner?"

"No, I won't. I have a home, a job, and things I need to do. I live too far away to keep commuting back and forth. I'm sorry you're confined to your condo, but it could be worse--you could still be in jail. Here's the information for how to do an on-line order for the grocery store. They'll deliver if you need anything."

"Will you come back tomorrow? I can't stand to stay here alone with nothing to do." He was actually whining.

"Grow up. You can probably do some office work on your computer, you have a television, books, etc. I'm not going to babysit you. Please, just stop it. I'm going now."

As he walked her to the door, he said, "Thank you for coming and do try to come tomorrow if possible."

"Bye, Ted," she said, giving him a little hug, and walking out the door.

As she exited the elevator, she looked around the silent parking garage. She took a breath and made a dash for her car, opening the door with the electronic key before she got to the car. She quickly slid in, locked the door, and looked around. It appeared that there was no one else in the garage. She relaxed, started her engine, and drove out to the street.

She was halfway home before she realized that she'd left the CDs she'd copied in the case with Ted's other CDs. Damn, she meant to bring those to give to Bill. She intended to give Gallagher the thumb drive. Maybe when she got home, she'd make another set of CDs. Hopefully Ted wouldn't discover them.

It started raining as she drove over the mountains. Summer weather on the coast was so changeable. In fact, that was one of the things she loved about beach living. Every day was different. In fact, often every hour's weather varied.

She sang along with Pink Martini and thought maybe she needed to get some new music for her car. Then she asked herself, why? She loved that group and thoroughly enjoyed accompanying them when she drove. Her mood was getting lighter as she got closer to home, even as the sky was getting darker. This looked like it could be a really stormy afternoon. Good time for coffee and a fire in her crow's nest, she thought. And maybe there'd even be some thunder and lightning.

Chapter Twenty-Seven

Sheba greeted Julie hungrily at the door. "My poor kitty," she said, bending down to pet her. "I'm sorry you've been alone so long and without any canned food. Glad I left you dry food which you apparently finished off." She looked at the empty bowl.

She fed Sheba, glanced at her blinking answering machine, but turned and carried her overnight bag and purse to her bedroom, dumping them on the floor.

She came back downstairs and reviewed her messages. Eleanor had called. She and Reverend Susan could come by later today if that was okay. Bill had phoned yesterday shortly after she left. He had business out of town and would be back tomorrow. He'd call her when he returned.

Well, that was that, she thought. She called Eleanor back and confirmed a time to meet Reverend Susan. Something positive to plan, she thought.

She climbed the stairs to her crow's nest, put on the coffee pot, and lit the fire. Just as she settled on the couch, lightning flashed and thunder roared. She was going to be able to witness her first big storm from this perfect viewing spot.

She sat enthralled, watching the storm move nearer until it seemed to be all around her. It was magnificent. This is what tourists came to the coast for during the winter, and today they were having one of the rarer summer storms.

After the storm blew through, she glanced at her watch and realized Eleanor and Reverend Susan would be by soon. She went downstairs, pulled some scones from the freezer, and made coffee. She would have a little something to offer them. She'd missed lunch, but she wasn't that hungry. This would do.

By the time they arrived, the rain had decreased to a drizzle. She welcomed them in, took their coats, and led them to the living room. She chatted with them briefly, then went to the kitchen to get the tray with the coffee and scones.

When she returned, Reverend Susan was looking out her window at the beach. She was tall, thin, and appeared to be in her late sixties. She wore her shoulder-length, gray-brown hair held back at the sides with clips. As she turned, Julie realized that she had one of those marvelous faces that contained mostly smiles and twinkling brown eyes.

"Quite a storm we had today," she said. "You must've had a really good view."

"Oh, I did. I was up in my crow's nest--the perfect place to be a storm watcher."

"So you enjoy storms, too," Reverend Susan said. "Then you'll really like the winter ones."

"Yes, we do get strong storms during the winter," Eleanor added. "This isn't a place for sissies. But, then, Julie doesn't appear to be a sissy with all that she's been going through."

"Yes, I understand you've had a rough time of it since you've moved in," Reverend Susan said. "You poor thing. But I think having a ceremony to cleanse your home and bless it is the perfect thing to do. Exactly what do you have in mind?"

The three of them sat down and chatted about the ritual, the sage smudging, selected the blessings, and chose a date--the following Saturday. Julie told them she'd make a guest list, which would be small, and she would have food and drink. Then she took Eleanor and Reverend Susan for a tour of the house.

"Oh my god," Reverend Susan said when they reached the crow's nest. "This is wonderful. I've always wanted a retreat like this myself. I think I'd be inspired to write great sermons here. We'll get the good spirits back for you."

When they were through admiring the room and the views, Julie walked them back down, thanked them both for coming, and said she'd give Reverend Susan a call if she thought of anything else. Otherwise the blessing was set for 5:00 Saturday followed by dinner.

Julie returned to her crow's nest, Sheba close behind. They settled on the couch, and she worked on her guest list. She didn't know that many people out here so it would be a small gathering: Eleanor, Jenn and Robbie, Reverend Susan and her husband Thad (she'd said he was an architect), Phil and Jon, and, of course Bill. Then she thought, why not add Jandy? She'd really liked her when they'd met at the bookstore, and she seemed the right kind of person to enjoy a house blessing. So, that would make ten, including herself. If everyone could attend.

She looked through the phone book and found that the owner of one of her favorite restaurants also did catering. Hopefully, she would be available on such short notice. Julie really couldn't settle down and cook with all that had been going on. A catered meal would be a lot simpler.

She called the restaurant. The owner was in, checked her calendar, and agreed she could put a meal together for a small group like that. She suggested cioppino, with a crispy salad, crusty french bread, and the house specialty, a wonderful chocolate mousse cake. The cioppino could go right on the stove to stay warm. It would be easy to serve. She would bring it by and set up at six, after the blessing and while the guests were eating appetizers and having drinks.

That was perfect for Julie. She'd have some hors d'oeuvres and wine before the ritual, do the blessing, nibble some more, hopefully out on the patio, and the caterer could set up the food in the kitchen. It felt good to be making some positive plans. In fact, for a few hours Julie had forgotten all about that awful thumb drive and making decisions about what she should do next. She hoped Gallagher or Bill would call soon.

As it turned out, neither phoned. She spent the evening watching old romantic films on TV as an escape and finally turned in to bed at midnight. Surprisingly, she slept well. Perhaps it was because she was home again, listening to the lullaby of the surf.

Morning broke with bright sun coming in. Quite a contrast from the day before. She would go for a beach walk later, she decided.

She fed Sheba, fixed coffee and breakfast, and sat outside to enjoy the nice weather. When she came in, she decided this would be a good time to invite her friends to her gathering on Saturday. She left a few messages--at Jenn and Robbie's and at Phil and Jon's. But she talked with Jandy, who was delighted to be invited. As she'd guessed, Jandy knew Reverend Susan and thought the ritual would be wonderful. Since Bill had said he was out of town, she decided to invite him when he called her.

She didn't have long to wait. Bill phoned and said he had a surprise for her if she was going to be around.

"A surprise," she answered. "Can't wait."

"I'll walk down in about twenty minutes."

"And I have a surprise for you, too," she said. "See you then."

While she was waiting for Bill, Jon called and said they'd be pleased to come on Saturday. Good. The party was shaping up. If she was lucky, all of this stuff should be over by then.

Bill knocked on the beach-side door, and she let him in. He hugged her lovingly.

"You look relaxed," he said. "Things must be going good for you."

"Not bad, and before I forget, I want to invite you to a party on Saturday. I'm having a house blessing followed by a dinner here. I'd like you to come. Do you know Reverend Susan? She's doing the blessing."

"Susan's a good person. I like her," Bill replied. "Sure, I'll be happy to come. And look what I found on the beach--your surprise." He pulled a giant, green fisherman's float out of his bag. "I know this isn't the same as the one that was broken, the designer one. But this is an original Japanese fisherman's float. It'll look great in here."

"Oh, Bill," Julie said taking the float and admiring it in the light. "I love it, especially the fact that it's real and has floated in the ocean for maybe months or years before reaching this coast. It has a history. I would love to know its story." She placed it on the shelf where the previous float had resided. "This is so special. Thank you." And she gave him another hug. He was so thoughtful.

They decided to go for a walk on the beach. She found a starfish and two shells to add to her treasures. Bill talked about a gallery he had visited while back east on his trip--the same gallery, he said, where Tina had worked while in college.

"An art gallery," Julie said. "I wonder how that fits into this scenario. You know, I found . . ." but was interrupted when Bill started gesturing out to sea.

"A whale," he said pointing. "Look." And she did.

The whale played offshore entertaining them for quite a while as they oohed and aahed.

"This is the first whale I've seen since moving in," she said. "I didn't think this was migration season."

"It's not. This is one of the whales that lives on our coast year round. We have some of those. But you'll really enjoy the migrations. Sometimes you see quite a few."

They continued their walk. She was still impressed by the sheer size of that leviathan.

When they returned to her house, he kissed her goodbye and said he'd see her tomorrow, if that was okay. He had things to do today.

She let him go without telling him about the thumb drive. She'd started to when he interrupted her to point out the whale, and afterwards they had been busy talking about whales and migrations.

She hadn't thought about it again until now. Should she call him? No, she'd wait until tomorrow. Maybe Gallagher would call. She really wanted to be straight with him this time.

She checked her phone machine. Damn, Gallagher hadn't called. She dialed the station. He was still out on personal business. She left another message. This time she said she'd found something she thought he'd be interested in. It was now up to him to get back to her.

After dinner, she climbed up to the crow's nest and began reading the book for the other club--women writers. They were reading Toni Morrison's *Beloved* which she'd read years ago, but needed to reread in order to participate in the discussion. This book would take real concentration.

Several hours later, she began dozing off in front of the fire, and decided to turn in early. She'd give Bill a call in the morning. She needed to unload this evidence with someone. If not Gallagher, then Bill.

Chapter Twenty-Eight

She shouldn't have thought of the thumb drive before she went to sleep. Her dreams were full of pitiful little faces begging her for help. Reading *Beloved* before bedtime hadn't helped either with all of the sadness and cruelty in its pages. Today she would get rid of the damn drive and hope that this evidence would help rescue some of those kids.

The more she thought about it, the more she decided Tina must have come across this while back east, had called the authorities, and had entered a witness protection program. She'd probably given them some of the evidence but kept the drive as insurance--to make sure the criminals would leave her alone, if they found her, and to make sure the Feds would stick to their word to hide and protect her.

So, they moved her out west. She somehow met Reggie, married him, and he probably introduced her to the gym where he worked out. She started going there, too. Not to become a body builder apparently, but to keep herself in shape. So what happened? Had somebody come in and recognized her from the east coast? Was the gym connected to the art gallery back in New Jersey? Did she recognize somebody there?

Wouldn't she have changed her appearance? She was a bottle-blond with long, shoulder-length hair. Who was she before? She hadn't asked for a picture from Bill. When he called her, she'd ask if he had Tina's high school yearbook or driver's license photo from New Jersey. She'd like to see if her theories made any sense. Actually, she'd run them by Bill, see what he thought.

Finally he called. She told him she had some evidence for him and asked him to bring a photo of Tina from the east coast.

He seemed surprised but said that he did have several, and he'd make copies for her.

He must have jogged down the beach to her house to make it there so quickly considering that he'd brought a picnic basket as well.

"What's this?" she asked, meeting him at the door.

"Oh, I thought that if you wanted to, we could look at your evidence and then go for that walk to the headlands we talked about. A small picnic would be perfect when we get there and give us the energy for a walk back. Now, what's the new evidence you've uncovered?"

"Just a minute," she replied. "First, did you bring the photos of Tina?"

"Yeah, I put them in top of the basket," he said, retrieving them. "So what do you think?" And he handed her the pictures.

"I have a theory that she was witness to crimes on the east coast through that gallery where she worked. Maybe the gallery was a front for child pornography and child sex trafficking."

Bill looked shocked and asked, "How on earth did you reach those conclusions?"

Julie studied the photos. "Look how different she looks here. Short, dark hair, heavier build. That's it. She joined the gym to keep weight off, dyed her hair blond, and grew it long. She was trying to look like a new person. I think she was in a Federal Witness Protection Program because she found out secrets about her bosses that were so horrifying she couldn't stay. She needed to be hidden away until she testified. I wonder if she got so terrified she fled the Witness Protection Program and married Denali to have another new identity. Wouldn't the case have gone to court by now?"

Bill looked at her curiously. "Granted, she changed her looks. But what makes you think she knew something about child pornography and the sex trade? That's a pretty big leap. And you think the gallery where she worked was involved?"

"Listen, Bill. I found something in the condo that helps bridge that gap--something that absolutely ties the owners of that gallery to some pretty awful stuff."

"What'd you find?" Bill demanded. "Show it to me."

"Slow down," she answered. "I'm planning to."

She pulled the thumb drive out of her pocket where she had put it that morning and showed it to him.

His eyes opened wide. "What . . . ?"

He started to grab it, but pulled back his hand and asked instead, "So what's on it? Why is this so important?"

"It has names, dates, photos of children. It's filled with incriminating evidence. My guess is she printed out the data she had for the Feds to get the ringleaders arrested, but kept the drive for insurance. But it looks like she's updated it since she moved here. She's found the same perverts here. I don't want to see it again, but you can look at it for yourself. I brought my laptop down. It's on the dining room table."

Bill attached the drive. As he looked at the screen, he began to groan. "This is terrible. Have you looked at all of it?"

"No, of course not. It was way too graphic with too much information to be taken in. It's so disturbing."

"Yes, it is," he said. "Does anyone else know about this? Ted? The police?"

"No, I couldn't show it to Ted. What good would that have done? And Gallagher hasn't returned my call. Hopefully, he'll be back in the office today."

"So, I'm the first one to view it?" Bill asked slowly, staring at her.

"Yes, don't you see? That's why Tina was killed. They killed her to find this. Only she gave them the wrong location, said it was in her office in the file folder box. They killed her so she couldn't testify. How did they find her? There has to be a connection with the gym." She began to feel hysterical.

"Hey," Bill said, putting his arms around her. "Calm down, sweetie. We can't do anything until Gallagher calls you. Let's go ahead and walk up the beach to the headlands. The fresh air will be good for both of us after seeing those horrible images. We'll walk, look at tide pools, eat, and come back. By then Gallagher should've called. What do you say?"

Bill was right. They couldn't do anything without Gallagher. He was only thinking of her and that calmed her.

"Thanks, Bill. I'm so glad someone else knows about the secret I've been carrying around. I appreciate your help. And trekking up the beach sounds much more enjoyable than just sitting here waiting for Gallagher to call."

"Okay," he said. "Grab a sweatshirt and let's go."

He picked up the picnic basket, and they went out the beach door. She carefully locked it behind them.

"Maybe I should hide the drive," she said.

"It'll be fine," he replied, "since nobody knows it's here."

As they walked along the shore, they looked for whales, but saw none. They tried to look for beach treasures. She found an agate she liked and put it in her pocket, but it was obvious that they were both troubled by what she'd found.

"I've got a question," she said. "When we went to Ted's condo, how did you know that the art on the walls was new, that he'd purchased it recently?"

Bill was unruffled. "Oh, that's easy. I'm familiar with the artist. I dabble in art a bit myself, and I recognized that these were newer works of his. Why do you ask?"

"Oh, just curious," she said shrugging. "Ted mentioned that he'd bought them several months before Tina died but that the gallery didn't install them until the day before her death. I was just wondering if the new art had anything to do with anything. I guess I'm stretching it."

"Yeah," Bill replied. "Not sure how that could be connected. Anyway, let's enjoy the view and the fresh air."

Julie couldn't believe how beautiful the headlands were. Above her the forest ran to the edge of the cliff and down it a few yards. Then there was a sheer drop-off to the beach below. Caves were interspersed in the cliffs, and a number of rocky outcroppings formed the basis for many tide pools. Bill was right. Exploring the beauty of this area would take her mind off the thumb drive and murder.

They wandered into the caves, and she imagined native Americans camped here after fishing. It was so serene, and due to its remoteness, they were the only ones enjoying it.

She breathed deeply and then turned to Bill saying, "What a magical place. Thank you so much for bringing me here."

He set the picnic basket down, hugged her, and murmured, "I knew it would be the perfect place."

Chapter Twenty-Nine

"Let's explore the tide pools before the tide comes in too much further and covers them," Bill suggested.

Julie answered, "As long as we don't go out too far. Slippery rocks scare me." She told him she'd had a fear of wet rocks ever since she'd slid and fallen while trying to cross stones over a small river as a kid. She'd almost drowned.

"It's okay, Julie," he said. "I'll take care of you. The best tide pools are just a little further out."

As she slipped on the rocks, Bill grabbed her hand to help steady her. That made her feel a bit more comfortable. Suddenly he had both her hands behind her and was forcing her out further onto the rocks toward the ocean.

"Stop it, Bill!" she cried. "This isn't funny. I really am frightened."

As she looked up at him, she saw no humor in his face at all.

"I'm not intending to be funny," he replied. "I'm sorry, Julie, but you know too much. If you looked further at the thumb drive, you would see my name mentioned. So far I've kept out of this mess because Tina hadn't seen the information about me. She only gave the Feds the earlier stuff. She probably couldn't stomach looking at the rest herself, just like you."

"You? You're involved in this horrible sex trade? How could you?"

"Relax, Julie," he said, holding her arms even tighter. "Those children had miserable lives where they came from. At least here they have shelter and food."

"You can actually justify what you do because they're housed and fed? I can't believe I slept with such a monster. I can't believe I was beginning to love you. What the hell does that say about me?"

"It says that you're gullible--that my charm worked on you. Do you really think I loved you? Come on, Julie. You're old enough to be the mother of most of the girls I date. Did you really think you were my type?" He laughed.

"It was so easy to seduce you," he continued. "You were hurting, vulnerable. Once I found out who you were, I knew that you could be the key to the evidence that Tina had not given us. I needed you."

"What about Vic?" she asked, as he pushed her further out on the rocks. "Was he one of yours? Did Tina recognize him at the gym?"

As terrified as she was, she had to keep him talking while she tried to think of a way out. At least she wasn't slipping any more. They paused while he bragged.

"Vic? Oh no, he was the undercover agent who'd been placed in the gym. It'd been under surveillance for quite some time. We were totally unaware of that. No, Vic just pretended to be a bad guy to try to get information from you. You were perfectly safe with him. However, because of you, I discovered his cover. I knew he wasn't working for our side, so he had to be a Fed. Thank you for sharing that information. With his cover blown, he disappeared."

"You killed Vic?" she asked.

"Why are you so surprised? I would have if I'd found him. But he was already long gone from the gym. I always try to get rid of liabilities. I learned that in Special Forces. If you don't want to be trapped, you have to be the better hunter. And I'm usually a damn good hunter."

"You're a damn good chameleon," Julie responded. He'd pushed her a few steps further. She avoided looking at the pounding surf as she tried to keep him talking. It was her only chance. "Why do you think Vic showed up the last time?"

"That's easy. He wanted the notebook. He really seemed to believe it would help his case. Also, he probably was afraid you might be in danger and was trying to get you out of the house. He knew you thought he was a gangster, so he continued to act like one. Would you've believed him if he'd told you the truth that day?"

"No, probably not," she said. "But who was behind my being hijacked to the brewery? Was that the Feds, too?"

"Oh, no. That was my boss. He believed you were becoming a liability and might tell Vic or the police about me. I tried to convince them that you might still have value for us, but he wanted you taken out. I was right. Fortunately, you got away, so now we have the real evidence we were after."

Julie swallowed. He talked about taking her out as if murdering her was just an ordinary chore that needed to be taken care of--like taking out the trash.

Staring at the incoming surf, she asked, "So what happened with Tina? Does the gym fit into this?"

"Well, actually you guessed right about the gym. It's one of our holdings. I happened to be there for a meeting when I spotted her. She didn't see me, but I recognized those eyes from back east. She may have totally changed her hair and thinned up her body a little, but those violet eyes were gorgeous. I'd seen her several times when I'd flown back there to the gallery, but we'd never met."

He tightened his grip on Julie as the water splashed around their ankles. The tide was coming in faster and the waves were getting bigger. Julie tried to keep focused on him and what he was saying.

He was obviously proud of what he'd done, so he continued verbally swaggering, the arrogant bastard.

"I was planning to seduce her at the gym, but then she came into my gallery downtown to see the paintings that Ted had preselected with my associate. Ted never met or saw me. She loved the art and arranged to get the paintings delivered a few months later when the show was over. Of course I knew those paintings were new in the condo. They'd been installed the day before she died and were there when I stabbed her. I'm surprised I let that slip. I'm usually pretty cautious. You have a good brain. Too bad you aren't going to be able to use it."

As Julie glanced over to her left, she saw two figures moving towards them in the distance. They kind of looked like a couple. As long as she could see them, they could see her. Hopefully, Bill wouldn't be able to do anything with witnesses nearby. She needed to keep him engaged so they could move closer.

"So when did you seduce her?" she asked. Bill pushed her another step toward the surf. She had to keep him talking.

"Oh, that was easy," he answered. "I asked her to come back the next day to look at some new art I was getting for some of their clients. It didn't take much. That was over two months ago. I charmed her as easily as I charmed you. She was lonely and frightened. She admired Ted, but I think she knew he couldn't protect her. I'm sure I appeared stronger. The longer we continued our affair, the more I tried to get her to tell me about herself, hoping she'd share her story, and I'd finally find the evidence. But no such luck."

Looking ahead, she saw that the ocean was swirling higher. The damn tide would be coming in. Bill tightened his grip and shoved her ahead one more step.

She turned her head to look him in the eyes. "That was your baby, wasn't it?"

"Right again," he answered. "Tina was going to tell Ted she was pregnant. I was afraid she'd tell him everything. And I wanted to locate the rest of the evidence. I knew she had something else. But she was a real trooper. She wouldn't reveal where she'd hidden it no matter what I did to her. I finally had to kill her without it, before Ted came back, so he'd look like the murderer. It worked, too."

"So, it didn't bother you that you killed your own child?"

"Do you really think it would bother me? Besides, until Ted was ruled out, I didn't know it was mine. Do you really see me as the daddy type?"

"No, someone who would make money off exploiting innocent children in the sex trade would not make a good father. Don't you have a conscience at all?"

"A conscience, my dear, does nothing but create problems. Fortunately, I've never had to worry about that."

And she realized that was true. He was a total narcissist focusing on only what brought him pleasure, power, and wealth--a real sociopath. How could she have thought she loved him?

Chapter Thirty

Her legs were getting wetter. They were far too close to the drop-off. She glanced past him, and he turned his head a bit too, holding her wrists tight with one hand, his other arm around her shoulders

He stopped talking as he saw the couple approaching, both in hoodies, huddled together.

"We've got company. Don't do anything silly," he said. "One small push and you're in the water being crushed against the rocks. I can always say you stumbled, and I tried to rescue you. Just let them walk and cuddle. They may not even see us."

He was right about that. They certainly weren't looking out toward the sea.

Please turn, she prayed. *Please stay out here.*

Then she asked Bill, "So when did she figure you out? When did she become a liability?"

"Oh, she never figured it out till I had the knife and was threatening her trying to get her to tell me where the evidence was hidden. Probably she realized then that I was going to kill her anyway, so what was the point in telling me? She died without saying a word."

"So what did you do? Just show up and wait around until Ted left?"

"Ted wasn't supposed to be home that afternoon. I was there to see Tina. However, when I arrived, he was just leaving the elevator. So I went on up. I moved quickly. I knew I had to get out of there in case he came back. And now he would be suspect for sure. That worked out well."

He looked kind of proud of that. Then he said, "I was surprised how hard it was to find the evidence. When I sent you off to the office, I figured that if it were there, then you and Ted would find it and bring it back to me, like you did the cellphone. I didn't count on Vic bumbling in there. I'm sure he had no idea you were in the office. He must have just grabbed something and got the hell out, playing the role of a thug."

"I still can't believe that Vic wasn't a bad guy. He sure looked like one, and you . . . ," she began.

"And I don't. That's what you were going to say, wasn't it? I get a lot of mileage with my good looks and charm."

He gripped her tighter as they both slid a little on the wet rocks and as he pushed her closer to the edge--too close--they couldn't go any further.

"What about Ted? Did you arrange for him to be stabbed?"

"Sure, only he was supposed to die. He was being prosecuted for Tina's murder. With him dead, the DA wouldn't look any further for the murderer. Case closed."

She looked at him in horror. Who was this man? Then she saw movement out of the corner of her eye. She turned her head. The couple was beginning to scramble onto the rocks, looking at the tide pools. Bill shifted a little watching them as well. His grip on her loosened as he tried to maintain his balance.

It was now or she'd never have a chance again, she thought. She'd never had much upper-body strength. But if she didn't try to push him in, he'd certainly kill her. Those damn slippery rocks. At least if she fell into the water, there'd be witnesses.

She took a deep breath, moved quickly, and threw Bill further off balance as she wrenched her wrists from him.

He wobbled and yelled, "You bitch." He flung out his arms trying to regain his footing.

This was her only chance. She lowered her head, giving him a hard head-butt. As he fell, seemingly in slow motion, he flailed his arms, grabbing at her, touching her sweatshirt, but not able to hold onto her or her shirt.

As she tried to recover her own balance, she watched him fall backward, head first, disappearing into the churning sea.

Julie teetered again, slipped on the rocks, and sat down hard. Thank god he hadn't taken her with him. She burst into tears.

Suddenly she was aware of the couple standing over her. Gallagher pulled his hoodie back as he sat down next to her and held her in a bear hug.

"It's okay," he murmured. "You're safe now."

Julie cried, "Oh my god. I think I just killed a man."

She looked into the roiling water, but Bill was nowhere to be seen.

"Couldn't have happened to a more deserving one," Gallagher replied.

"Please get me off these damn rocks," she sobbed, as the tide continued to rise, splashing them more with each new wave. Soon the rocks would be under water.

He helped her stand and hung onto her tightly as they moved carefully over the slick rocks to the sand near the caves where she collapsed. She watched as the other half of the hoodie couple, an officer she'd seen at the station before, went further out onto the far edge of the rocks to look for Bill while calling for assistance on his radio.

"There he is!" he shouted, pointing to a body that slammed repeatedly against the boulders further out in the ocean.

Gallagher and Julie stood up to look more closely. Bill's bloodied body was being thrown forcefully against the rocks. The waves would pull him out and dash him in again and again. There seemed to be more blood than body. He had to be dead. Julie closed her eyes.

The other officer radioed for assistance again. Apparently there'd been some officers waiting nearby. They drove up the shoreline in several jeeps. But as they approached and climbed out on the rocks, there was nothing anyone could do. If they went into the water, they'd be dead, too. The sea was too violent.

"He can't possibly be alive," Gallagher yelled to them. "Keep a crew out here and see if he washes up anywhere close enough so that his body can be pulled in."

Turning to Julie, he said, "This has been an awful day for you. I'm so sorry you had to go through this."

"Do you know what he was?" Julie spat. "He was the most horrible kind of monster, and I thought I loved him? What's the matter with me?"

Gallagher tried to comfort her. "How would you know? You don't live in that world."

"Didn't live in that world. Oh, I've seen too much of it now. I can never forget about this kind of evil. Wait until you see the thumb drive."

"I've seen the CDs," he answered. "Ted called this morning and demanded that I come straight over. He'd put a CD in his computer not realizing it wasn't one of his. When he looked at it, he called me immediately. We saw enough to be concerned about you, especially when my office finally told me you had evidence for me. Then I realized that you must have the original. Also, that CD held the code for her notebook. We can begin to make sense out of the stuff she was observing at the gym."

He shook his head. "The Feds had given us a few hints, but they keep their cards close to their chests. It wasn't until we discovered who Tina really was that we started asking hard questions, and they finally gave up a little information. No one told us that Bill might be involved, but the fact that Ted said he'd hired him, something neither of you had ever mentioned, plus the fact that when we got to your house, you were heading up the beach with Bill, put us in a stealth mode."

"You and the other officer were a convincing couple in the distance," Julie said, laughing for the first time that afternoon.

"Don't tell his wife," Gallagher replied with a smile. "We knew we had to look innocuous so Bill wouldn't do anything crazy. Thank god you pushed him before he shot or pushed you. There was only going to be one winner there out on the rocks. I'm glad it was you."

"I don't even kill spiders," Julie cried. "And I killed a man."

"No," Gallagher said. "You saved your own life and partially destroyed evil. He was a major player, and now we'll get the other guys with the evidence from that drive and notebook."

Epilogue

It was late Saturday evening. Her guests had just left. There were nine instead of ten. Bill, of course, didn't make it. She'd invited Gallagher who'd thanked her but told her that new age stuff wasn't his thing. She'd understood. She couldn't really see him there, anyway.

The house blessing and cleansing had been beautiful. She hoped that the awful images of those poor children would begin to fade as well. At least they were no longer in her computer or her house.

Bill's body had finally dashed against the rocks high enough with the incoming tide that he could be pulled in. Gallagher said he would've been unrecognizable if they hadn't known it was him. So Bill was dead. She was still confused that her internal radar had led her astray with him, but then realized she'd always had a few doubts that she'd refused to honor.

Here at the gathering, everyone knew about the case. It had broken big in the papers with follow-up stories that morning on some of the rescued children. That was the one good thing to come out of all this mayhem--some of the children's lives were saved. She hoped it wasn't too late to save their emotional selves, too.

Reverend Susan had said just the right things to wash away the evilness as she smudged sage in all the corners of the rooms on all three floors. Jandy was supportive, hugging her and saying, "Girl,

I can't believe you went through all of this. If you need a friend, please drop in the book store for coffee, conversation, or just a hug."

Phil and Jon were bragging about Jon's part in rescuing her. She didn't have the heart to tell them that he'd rescued her from a federal agent pretending to be a thug. Let them believe Jon was a hero. She'd appreciated Jon's willingness to take a risk and rescue her. He was her knight, all right.

And actually it turned out that the "Boy Scout" who'd come to her aid her was a Fed, too, not one of Bill's employees. He'd arranged with Vic to rescue her, hopefully after Vic scared some information from her. However, she had nothing to give him. She was surprised that government agents could behave in such a frightening way. Gallagher'd said that apparently they played a little loosey-goosey in high stakes cases like this.

Bill'd had a tail on her who saw it all happen--that's how he knew about it. Bill's tails and security, of course, weren't for her safety but to keep him informed about what she was doing. It'd been so overwhelming.

And Tina, poor Tina, had been in a Witness Protection Program. Apparently she was never married to Denali but pretended to be as part of her cover. Their split was never a problem since he'd never been her lover, just a protector hired by the Feds. When she left him for Ted, he'd hung around a bit at the gym, participated in the DNA test, and then disappeared.

And yes, she'd found more information at the gym. They'd never know exactly what it was since the Feds weren't talking, but apparently it was going to be enough to convict most of those thugs. The thumb drive was the key. They could now prosecute even without Tina as a witness.

She thought about Eleanor. That evening Eleanor had embraced her and said, as only a Brit can, "I'm completely gob-smacked! I knew there were strange going-ons at your house, but I had no idea you were involved in stopping an international child sex ring. My god. You are so strong."

So strong, she thought now as she reclined on the couch in her peaceful crow's nest, listening to the surf.

She guessed she was. Ted couldn't believe she'd gotten to the bottom of all this. His bracelet was now off, and he wanted to come for a visit. She put him off. She hadn't told him about the party. He needed to build his own life, separate from hers.

Now, at last, she could become the person she'd hoped she'd find at the beach. She couldn't wait to begin to enjoy life. And she'd always have this beautiful room, this crow's nest, to come home to.

Acknowledgements

First, I wish to thank the National Novel Writing Month program which happens every November. I went on-line and registered for this now international program in 2010, beginning my odyssey of completing 50,000 words by the end of November. Having to daily log my word count kept me moving forward. This was the first time I wrote continuously, not going back to edit, not knowing where my characters were headed, and not even realizing it would be a mystery until the fourth chapter when I wrote a murder into the story. It was an amazing process.

I let my book sit for a good six months. Finally, I picked it up, read it, and realized I was pretty proud of this first draft. So I began rewriting it--building consistency, developing characters, etc. After my third rewrite, I attended a retreat with my friends from the Inland Area Writing Project in Riverside, California. Friend and author, Marilyn Donahue, read the whole manuscript in one night. She wrote some comments and felt that I should proceed with the book. I thank her for taking the time that weekend to read my work and encourage me. Friend Karen Coates also read it and gave me a few tips, especially when dealing with technology. My daughter, Sarah Brown, gave me more solid advice. Additionally, my writers group, CC Writers (Creative Crone Writers), have suffered through numerous chapters and rewrites at our bi-monthly meetings. I thank them for all of their help and suggestions--Pattie Anderson, Jacquie Beveridge, Denise Dee, Mary Nulty, and Sharon Stiles.

Without the assistance of Mike Foley, my writing teacher for the past ten years, who edited a late draft for me, I doubt I would have completed it. His attention and care are spot on, and I thank him for all of his work with me over the years. Amazingly, we have never met in person, but have done all our work together through the internet and by mail.

For the last close readings, I thank Sharon Stiles, Pattie Anderson (both CC Writers), and Sally Lineback, a childhood friend. They diligently tried to find the last of the punctuation errors, typos, etc. Any errors that remain are totally my responsibility. But I feel blessed to have had the support of so many writing friends. It may not take a village to write a book, but it takes the village to get it into acceptable published form. Thank you all.

The cover is perfect thanks to Pattie Brooks Anderson's beautiful art. She captured the house I'd only imagined. The original inspiration was a townhouse where I'd attended an open house in the early eighties. She turned that remembrance into the visual depiction of the home I created in this story.

Made in the USA
Lexington, KY
20 January 2014